THE

TUSKS

OF

EXTINCTION

Also by **RAY NAYLER**

The Mountain in the Sea

Ray Nayler

THE
TUSKS
OF
EXTINCTION

TOR PUBLISHING GROUP
New York

THE TUSKS OF EXTINCTION

Copyright © 2023 by Ray Nayler

A Tordotcom Book
Published by Tom Doherty Associates / Tor Publishing Group
120 Broadway
New York, NY 10271

www.tor.com

Tor® is a registered trademark of Macmillan Publishing Group, LLC.

The Library of Congress Cataloging-in-Publication Data is available upon request.

ISBN 978-1-250-85552-7 (hardback)
ISBN 978-1-250-85553-4 (ebook)

Our books may be purchased in bulk for promotional, educational, or business use. Please contact your local bookseller or the Macmillan Corporate and Premium Sales Department at 1-800-221-7945, extension 5442, or by email at MacmillanSpecialMarkets@macmillan.com.

First Edition: 2024

Printed in the United States of America

0 9 8 7 6 5 4 3 2 1

For Anya and Lydia

THE

TUSKS

OF

EXTINCTION

ONE

DAMIRA FOLLOWED THE blood down the hill. The ground here was soft with upwelling water. Rivulets reflected the sun through blades of grass. Her feet sank a few centimeters into the upper layer of soil before meeting the spongy mat of root web.

She could not see much blood, but the pathway of blood-scent was clear. Touching her trunk to the Jacobson's organ in the roof of her mouth conjured the mammoth she called Koyon—his shy, lumbering form, his tattered right ear, his mournful, hairy head.

Koyon's eyes were amber, not the dark earthen color of most of the others. Beautiful eyes, long lashed and soulful. Damira remembered when the herd drove him off two summers ago. For weeks, he had trailed them at a distance, trumpeting desperately when any of them turned to look at him, winding his trunk through the scent-path of mother and kin. She had not seen when he finally turned and went away. She had tried not to look in his direction too much: it only prolonged the agony of the driving off, of the necessary separation of the males from the herd that was a part of their adolescence. Some wandered off themselves, some had to be charged, butted, shoved away by the matriarchs into their solitary adult lives.

The next summer season she saw him with Yekenat, the oldest and largest of the bulls. Yekenat was massively tusked, tall and thick through the chest, tawny pelted. Koyon trailed the larger male at a respectful distance, watching his mentor tear grass from the steppe. When the matriarchs and his shaggy cousins passed, he swung his trunk to trace their scent on the wind.

But he did not approach. He, like the others, had come to understand the proper order of things.

Damira heard the flies. The sound was weaker than it had been on the banks of the Ewaso Ng'iro . . .

DAMIRA HEARD THE sound of the flies and smelled the stench of death in the air. She hesitated at the base of the hill, shifted her rifle from one shoulder to the other. Wamugunda halted beside her. They had seen the vultures in the sky. They knew what was over the red earth hill. Neither of them wanted to see it for themselves. But the sound was almost worse than the sight: the enormous buzz of death. The hum of destruction. A hot exhalation of rot hit them. Wamugunda gagged. He spat in the red dirt, unashamed.

Damira did not gag. She would not let herself. If she did, she would vomit.

She pushed forward, over the crest of the hill.

There were eight of them here. There were six adults, all females. There was an adolescent bull that must have been only a season or two away from being pushed out of the herd. And there was a calf, no more than a few days old.

The flies swarmed the mutilated faces of the matriarchs and the adolescent bull. Their trunks were hacked away, their tusks gouged out, their feet chopped off.

Musa was already there. He stood with the farmer who had found them, both of them smoking. To ward off the stench. And to give them something to do while they waited, besides staring at the slaughter.

"Shot from the air," Musa said. "Probably an ex-military drone—a flying machine gun, radar cloaked and silenced. They came in later on ATVs to harvest the tusks. It's one of the big operations. Well-funded. They set a booby trap, by the way, for us. An IED—tripwire in the brush there next to the adolescent bull. Mortar round. So, they send us their regards. There may be more IEDs around. I checked best I could, but be careful."

Damira stood at the edge of the destruction, looking down at the last of the victims.

The pink calf lay, untouched by poachers, as if she had fallen asleep. Her rosy ears were still translucent. She had stayed with the buzzing ruins of her mother and her clan, and lay down to die just a few days after coming into the world.

The individual elephants slaughtered were lost in the numbers—the elephants butchered by the thousands, cut down by ivory hunters until there were almost none left in the wild. Seeing the individual acts of butchery was a reminder that every killing of an elephant was, like the elephant itself, enormous. A towering act of human cruelty.

But the numbers were not what Damira thought of when she later remembered those years of struggle along the Ewaso Ng'iro. And the mutilated adults and adolescents were not what she thought of, either. What stayed with her most was the baby, pink and newly born, that had remained with its mother until the end.

The elephant calf became a symbol for her of the entire lost war against the poachers, and against the system that supported them. Whenever she needed a reason to continue, the calf was there, behind the lids of her eyes.

And she did not give up. None of them gave up. Not her, and none of the rangers who fought the poachers.

Musa looked up into a sky already turning white-blue with the heat of late morning.

"Our day will come, and the corpses of the poachers who did this will be scattered by the banks of the Ewaso Ng'iro, covered in flies."

"Yes," Wamugunda said, "our day will come."

"Our day will come," Damira said. But when she spoke the words, her voice was too faint to be heard over the buzzing swarm.

In less than a year, Musa would be dead, killed by a sniper at base camp along with three other rangers.

Two years later, Wamugunda would be killed at the wheel of

his Range Rover, by an artillery shell IED placed along one of the national park's dirt roads.

And Damira was murdered a year after that.

THE TRAIL OF blood wound around the base of a kurgan and into a slight depression fanned by rivulets of glacial meltwater. Yekenat and Koyon lay side by side, no more than fifteen meters apart. The flies swirled up and then settled again on what had been the heads of the two mammoths. Only their tusks had been taken, but the cutting away had been done in haste, their skulls hacked open to get every inch of ivory. There was nothing left of Koyon's mournful face, or Yekenat's powerful head, the tusks growing thicker at the base as he, one of the first mammoths to be reborn, entered into his middle years.

There were boot-prints in the soft earth. No tire tracks, but strange hoof-like imprints where the grass was thin. And, of course, the brass of the shells, littering the steppe. It was all recent: this had happened today. The corpses had barely begun to rot.

When Damira returned to her clan they sniffed at her, drawing their trunks over the smell of death that saturated her pelt, walking in slow circles as they touched the death-smell to the tops of their mouths. The calves moved closer to their mothers, nuzzling their sides and grasping with their trunks at their parents' hairy pelts.

Kara, Koyon's mother, stood and swayed, her eyes closed. The others stroked their trunks along her sides and comforted her with low rumbles.

But Damira felt no sadness. None at all. There was no room for it in her. All she could think of was Musa looking up into the sky.

"Our day will come, and the corpses of the poachers who did this will be scattered by the banks of the Ewaso Ng'iro, covered in flies."

Damira's furious trumpeting startled the others out of their mourning. But soon, they all had caught the feeling, pacing and flapping their ears, mock-charging as if the poachers were there around them.

TWO

"ONCE, WHEN MY Nenets mother was a small child, her family was moving their reindeer herd from one pasture to another. As they were fording a river, my grandfather saw something strange in the mud on the bank. Like a mass of hair, with great horns curving out from it. He took a closer look, and then forbade anyone in the family to go near it. But they all slowed their reindeer and stared as they went past. My mother told me how its teeth showed on one side of its hairy skull in a terrible grin, and the great horns came not out of the top of its head, but out of the front of its face.

"It was a mammoth, exposed by a spring thaw and floodwater cutting into the banks of the river. Later that night, after they had set up camp, my grandmother asked my grandfather why they were not allowed to touch it or even approach it. He told her it was a servant of *Nga*, master of the frozen underworld. It had tried to escape through a hole into the middle world, the world where we live, and had become trapped between. To touch it, or even to go near it, was bad luck—it would put a curse on the family. Many Nenets who had disturbed the creatures from the underworld ice died from disease or went mad, he said. Whole villages could be destroyed."

"Did she say how big its tusks were?" Dmitriy asked. "I bet someone made a fortune off that 'monster'—and if they went mad, it was in a Moscow *banya* surrounded by blondes."

The mechanic who had been speaking, a man named Myusena, just shook his head and returned to his bowl of rice and fish.

Dmitriy nudged Svyatoslav. "We touched plenty of monsters from the underworld last year, without any madness. Right, son?"

Svyatoslav thought of the expedition he had taken with his father last year, hunting for mammoth tusks in the thawing permafrost along a muddy, freezing river. He thought of the wounds torn in the earth by the miners' hoses, the men in rubber hip-waders crawling into the gaping holes, chipping fragments of bone, teeth, and skulls from the ice.

They had found no tusks, but at one point the melting ice ceiling of a hole collapsed. One of the men was buried forever in that filth. Afterward, the others realized they only knew his first name. Nobody could even remember where he'd said he was from. There was nobody to tell about his death.

The whole expedition had been a blur of drunkenness and chaos. On the way back downriver, one of the boats foundered and sank. The "team," bickering and fighting the whole way, had to cram into the other boat and labor home, dangerously taking on water while the men passed a bottle around.

All they had to show for the trip was one complete steppe bison skull, which they cleaned and mounted on the front of the boat.

Later, while the men were drunk in some nowhere town and Svyatoslav was huddled in the hotel room with a pillow over his head to keep out the sounds of the things happening in the hallway and in the adjacent rooms, someone stole the skull. That left them with nothing to show for the trip at all.

"I think your grandfather was right," Svyatoslav said to Myusena. "The creatures of the underworld are cursed, and terrible things happen to people who disturb them."

Myusena looked up at him. Svyatoslav could not tell if it was a look of gratitude or suspicion or contempt: the six men in the tent were all drunk. Their slack faces in the colorless LED light of the tent's lantern were unreadable.

Only Svyatoslav was sober. He never drank. This made him suspicious to everyone, almost feared. But the one thing his father did not press on him was alcohol. Throughout all of it, he'd never tried to pour Svyatoslav a glass.

"Here's a toast, then, to curses!" Dmitriy said.

Svyatoslav did not hear the rest. Wrapping his plastidown blanket around his shoulders, he left the tent.

The drone mules were about thirty meters away. They stood with their stumpy heads lowered, completely motionless. Svyatoslav could never get used to the drone mules: every time he approached them, he expected them to shift their weight or twitch a tail, like real mules. But they looked nothing like real mules. And when activated, their movements were more spider-like than mule-like.

Svyatoslav retrieved his drone kit from one of the saddlebags. He found himself making a wide circle around the last mule, with its strapped-down load of four long, curving tusks, still spattered and smeared with blood.

The mules were Myusena's—they were the only reason he was on this expedition. When Dmitriy and his hunting buddies were planning the trip, they had first thought of using ATVs, as they usually did. But ATVs were loud, and could be easily tracked. So they had found Myusena, the muleteer and mechanic, and convinced him to come along. The group had left their ATVs beyond the boundaries of the reserve, hidden in a copse of larch, under branches and needles, along with their terminals, shut off and cloaked in a Faraday bag.

The mules were nearly silent, no louder than real mules on the trail.

But silence was in short supply. Listening to the drunken laughter of the men in the tent, Svyatoslav wondered how far that sound carried. The reserve was huge, and remote, and nobody had ever poached in it before that they knew of, but Svyatoslav looked up into the sky and expected to hear, from out of the starred dark, the buzz of a patrol drone. Nothing as valuable as the mammoths could be left unguarded. There would be camera traps—and worse.

But not yet. And maybe they would escape. Maybe they would get out. It was three days' march to the edge of the reserve. To the ATVs. Then two more days, if the weather held, to where the battered old UAZ van waited beside an abandoned hunter's cabin. Load the tusks in, sell them to a contact—the sum it was rumored they could get for them was unbelievable. The market was hot. The tusks of a mammoth brought back from extinction had never been sold before. But already, there were buyers waiting.

The prices were fantasy numbers. Enough for all of them to retire on, if it worked out. Enough to build a life on. In Moscow, sure—but even farther off, in places wreathed in fantasy. London. New York. Theoretical cities no one ever returned from. Places that might have been other planets.

It did not seem possible, to live through all of this. To actually get out of here. To leave this life behind. The stench of poachers' tents, the smeared faces of drunken men, the crushed limbs and drownings and accidental gunshot wounds.

Svyatoslav was sixteen, and he had known nothing else for years now. Before his mother died, there had been none of this. There had only been the grim apartment blocks of the city—the dim stairwells full of chipped paint and trash, the flowers of frost blooming on the window of his bedroom, the rusty playground. And then his mother in the hospital, thin as if she were withdrawing into her own skeleton—thin as if her bones were breathing in her flesh and consuming it.

Up to that moment, his father had been a rare thing in their home—sweeping in loud and chaotic, accompanied by other men, by the corpses of animals. Scheming and oiling his rifle. Not a parent—a myth. An anticipation, an encounter, a departure.

He was thirteen when his mother died. After she went into the hole hacked in the frozen ground, he hunted with his father. He had nowhere else to go.

They said his father was the best hunter for a thousand kilometers, but all Svyatoslav saw was chaos, filth, destruction. Hunting didn't seem like a skill: you armed yourself, you went out into the woods, and you waited. And then you killed something that did not have any of the tools you had.

The waiting was simple enough—wind direction, blinds, concealment. You could learn it in a season. The real advantage was the gun, and knowing how to use a gun was also nothing to be proud of. Any idiot could use one. Most of the people who used them were idiots. Svyatoslav had always known how to use one. During his father's rare appearances in his early childhood, there had always been time to learn, pegging cans with the little gun his father had also learned on. Shooting was just muscle action, as easy as walking.

What was harder, for the hunters, was to stay sober. To stay alert and together, against the backdrop of endless taiga, the swarming mosquitoes and the swamps sucking at your boots, the slaughter of creatures for profit. To go to sleep at night, not stay up drinking and then stagger through the expedition in a destructive haze. It was because of the drinking that the expeditions ended in disaster, injury, death.

It seemed at first like they drank out of boredom—but really it was out of disgust. They drank to throw a curtain of intoxication over the filth, the stench of themselves, the violence of their actions, the futility of it all.

And it *was* futile. They were often robbed by gangsters—who were nothing but other desperate men. But even that wasn't always necessary: they found other ways to lose it all. They invested what they gained in fraudulent schemes, blew it all gambling, dropped it out of a pocket on a bender, gave it to a lover who skipped town.

None of the poachers creeping through the taiga or the mammoth tusk hunters blasting gouges into the permafrost with hoses ever got rich: all of them went into the earth early, one way or another. All of them went into the earth with nothing to show for it.

Into the frozen underworld with *Nga,* perhaps. That explanation was as good as any.

Svyatoslav slipped the headset on and released the drone, a

thing the size of a bumblebee, and no heavier, watching from its perspective as it spiraled into the air, looking back at the mono-chrome green thermal image of himself looking up at the drone. The mules barely registered, just thin bleeds of heat around their joints like spots against the darker earth, little hotter than the grass—but he could make out the grass, subtly warmer than the earth around it, and a thermal spring near the camp that they had not known about, heat-green veins along the ground.

Somewhere out there in the dark, in the green of this false sight, were the two mammoths they had killed. Svyatoslav wanted to see them, their bulk barely visible against the grass they had fallen onto. Their heat fading. They would be peaceful, seen from the drone's perspective. They would be part, already, of the land around them.

And maybe that final sight of them, at peace now, would erase the memories of the kill in his head: the terrible trumpeting of the mammoths rearing in pain; the fear in the eyes of the smaller one as bullet after bullet thudded into him and he charged clum-sily, uncertainly, in one direction and then another until finally he sank to his knees.

The older, larger one had caught sight of the hunter Sergei and charged him, and for a moment Svyatoslav had thought that was it for Sergei, who tripped and fell. Sergei scrambled to his feet and then tripped again, like someone running from a monster in a movie.

But Svyatoslav's father put a high-caliber bullet into the mam-moth's eye. It crashed down in a pink mist, sighing its life out with a moan like the earth's protest against everything humans stood for.

Svyatoslav helped with the detusking. He felt completely shut off—almost peaceful, void of any emotion at all, hacking into the great skulls to free the long, curving tusks.

But then, as the others were lugging the tusks and strapping them with thick tie-downs to the drone mule, Svyatoslav went behind the kurgan, put his face in the grass, and wept. Wept terribly, choking back sound, shoving his face into the grass and earth. Wept until he shook, and his entire body felt empty and drifting.

Svyatoslav wrapped his plastidown blanket around himself and brought the drone in a wide circle, arcing over the green land of drone perception, curving down toward the tent, which shone like a sack of coals, each of the six men inside a blurry, brighter spot. The drone hovered and listened.

"It's not that I won't let him drink," Dmitriy was saying. "It's that he's never wanted to. And you know how it is—once you've started, it's how you will finish. I don't want that for him. I want him to finish in another way. Far from here."

"Beyond thrice-nine lands in the thrice-tenth kingdom," Myusena said.

Drunken laughter.

"Something like that. You know your Russian folktales well for a Nenets."

"My father wasn't Nenets. He was Russian. In fact, he was a man like you."

"Like me?"

"Yes. A man who thought he could pass the good on to his son without the bad."

There was silence in the tent, for a moment.

Then one of the other men said, "He's right, Mitya. All our fathers were the same."

"Well, let's drink to our fathers then. They wanted the best, but it turned out the same as always."

Laughter.

Svyatoslav switched the drone into its autoreturn routine. He took the headset off and lay down on the ground. It was warm enough to sleep out here. He wouldn't have to return to the stinking tent. The stars blazed above him. The Milky Way was wide and dusty as a road. The drone settled down to the grass beside him with a whir.

That smell. He brought his hands up to his face. The copper

smell never washed out. It cut through everything else. Every time he came back from one of these trips, he stank of blood. At first fresh, and then congealed and sweet-rotted, the stench haunting him even after a hot shower. Sometimes it came from nowhere, weeks later, as he was standing in line at a store or drifting off to sleep, as if it had been preserved inside him and exhaled through his pores.

"Never again," he said aloud. "I'll never have to do it again."

But at once the thought was contradicted by another one.

It wouldn't work. They wouldn't get the money. They wouldn't get out.

The hunters all went into the earth early, one way or another. Into the frozen underworld with *Nga*.

THREE

"WHAT WILL I feel?" Damira asked the woman in the white lab coat behind the bank of terminals. The woman had come into the room without introducing herself, and begun adjusting equipment. A graduate student or postdoctoral resident with the project.

"People report different things. Some say they feel nothing at all. Others say the scan brings up memories. That it somehow brushes up against them and brings them back to consciousness. They see their lives. Memory by memory, before them."

"Like when you die."

"Yes. That's what they say, right? That's the superstition."

Damira hoped there would be nothing.

She had not agreed, at first, to be backed up. She received the notice on her terminal to report to the Institute, and ignored the summons. She had not come back to Russia for this—had not come back to take part in the Institute's experiments.

She had come back to get more support for the war against the poachers in Kenya. That is what it was—a war. She called it a war because that was the word she thought might get people's attention. And she called it a war because just like every war, it existed only for the people it was happening to. Like every war, it was particular to a place and time. Everywhere else, it could be ignored.

In Moscow, life continued as if nothing was happening at all. As if tens of thousands of elephants were not dying. As if the rhino were not already nearly extinct, surviving only in test tubes and zoos. People in Moscow drank fancy Western coffees at three times the price paid in the West and wandered, blank-faced, down Stary Arbat's cobblestones, lost in self-improvement feedstreams. People were certain that, no matter what the problem was, it could not touch *them*. People were certain *someone else* would fix it, if they even thought of the war at all.

She had walked down Stary Arbat herself, that same morning. Had tried to be normal, for one sliver of time. She had stopped for a moment in front of a yoga studio and watched the slow movement of sweating people inside turning from one pose to another, and sipped her overpriced coffee, and tried to be a person she was not.

But the way they moved, slow and certain and aligned, even briefly, with the world around them and with one another made her think of the slow, sure grace of her elephants. They were dying *right now*. She was here on the Arbat and they were dying *right now*, their numbers dwindling toward extinction and every death a hole torn in the world.

She tossed half the coffee in the trash, feeling guilty for the waste. But pouring it into her body was just as much of a waste.

A few moments later a voice call came in.

"You have to answer the summons, you know."

It was Yelena. They had gone to graduate school together. Now she was with the Institute. Not a part of the Mind Bank project. What was the latest thing she was working on? Damira did not know.

"Did they put you up to calling me?"

"No, I saw your name on the list and knew you would be trying to ignore it. But you can't. They'll put a hold on your passport. The Duma passed a law. They can strip you of your grant money, do whatever they like. They can even put you in jail, and make you do it. Come by and get it over with."

"I'm thinking it over."

"Really. They won't let you leave. I saw you on the streams yesterday, talking about what is happening in Kenya. You have important things to get back to—don't let this stand in your way."

"Have *you* done it?"

"You kidding? The Mind Bank is for geniuses and heroes.

Experts in their fields—like you. Our National Intellectual Wealth, I think they are calling it. Not people who sit around in labs making fruit flies glow in the dark. Nobody's going to be looking to bring *us* back from the dead."

"ISN'T THERE ANY way for us to be . . . anesthetized?"

"No," the woman in the lab coat said. "You have to be awake. But it doesn't hurt. And it doesn't require anything from you at all. You don't have to concentrate or anything. All you have to do is relax and let it happen. You probably won't feel much: most people don't. Some report a tingling or some other pleasant sensation."

"Or the memories."

"Yes, the memories. But most people say those are nice. I saw you on the streams, by the way—it's terrible what is happening to the elephants. And it's good you are forcing people to listen. It's incredibly brave of you, standing up to the international cartels like that."

But people weren't listening. And Damira sometimes felt she should stop talking about it. It wasn't bravery, she thought, it was love. A desperate love that wouldn't let her allow it to happen.

"When will it start?"

"We've already started. Do you feel anything?"

She did not. But then, she saw—very clearly, as if it were in the room with them—a stuffed elephant toy. It lay on its side, as if dropped on the table. On the surface of the table, which had become a scratched linoleum floor.

Her first elephant.

It was her uncle Timur who gave it to her, on one of his returns from a month-long shift in the oil fields of the Timan-Pechora Basin.

Timur was her mother's older brother. He was Damira's favorite uncle. His month-long disappearances made him mysterious. She waited for his return for the entire time he was gone.

Every knock on the door of their little wooden house in the Tatar neighborhood of Tomsk was Timur. Finding it was not him, she would flee from the visitor in disappointment.

He brought her something every time he came back. The elephant was one of those gifts. Once Timur saw the joy the little stuffed elephant brought her, elephants became the theme of his gifts: first a few more stuffed toys, and then books. *Babar,* in Russian translation. And, as she got older, books on real elephants.

Strange, how a life forms from those incidents. How an adult can have so much impact upon the path a child takes. How an adult could give a child a gift without knowing what pathways it would open, what potentials it might reveal. Perhaps the first gift was only happenstance—the object that was available, the only thing left at the store—or simply the thing that had caught Timur's eye or some unnamable and unimportant reason. And from there it became a game for him—finding something related to elephants for a little girl who was always waiting for him.

Timur had no children of his own. He spent half his life among men like himself, in barracks in the Arctic, at work in the oil fields. He spent the other half in his apartment—a place she visited with her mother only once, in all those years. Only once: the day they found out Timur had been killed.

Damira was twelve. They went with a locksmith and a fistful of stamped permissions, and stood in a cold stairwell for five minutes while the man cursed abominably over the lock, then finally got it open.

And inside there was nothing at all. No—that wasn't right: there were things—furniture, clothing, a jar of pickles in the refrigerator. There was a souvenir magnet from Kamchatka, a picture on the wall of a mountain range, a battered leather portfolio filled with the documents a person needed to exist in the world.

But what Damira remembered was that there was nothing. The apartment was warm from the central heating—even a bit stuffy, as nobody was around to regulate the temperature by opening a window now and then. It was waiting for his return, but in it was nothing that *expressed* what Timur was like. Nothing that seemed to belong to him as a *particular* person. The person who faithfully, every month, found something related to elephants and brought it to his niece. It was as if, in a sense, that act—the repetition of that small act of giving a gift to her—was all that Timur was.

"He needed someone to take care of him," Damira's mother said, wiping a finger along the dust on the top of the refrigerator. "We all do."

She remembered Timur sitting on the edge of her bed. Her mother had gone to the store, leaving Timur to watch over her for a few hours. The evening light poured, salmon-colored, in through the bedroom window. He turned the page, cleared his throat, and began:

"In the High and Far-Off Times the Elephant, O Best Beloved, had no trunk. She had only a blackish, bulgy nose, as big as a boot, that she could wriggle about from side to side; but she couldn't pick up things with it. But there was one Elephant—a new Elephant—an Elephant's Child—who was full of 'satiable curiosity, and that means she asked ever so many questions . . ."

Later Damira discovered that, in the original book, the Elephant's Child was *he*. Her uncle had changed it to *she* for her.

Because I am the Elephant's Child.

DAMIRA SHIFTED HER great bulk in the darkness. She turned her head to look at the others, lined up behind her. Closest to her was Kara, whose head lolled, hanging tiredly. Again and again Kara touched her trunk to the top of her mouth. She was remembering Koyon. The smell of her son. Damira had seen the gesture before. She knew it from her own self—her mammoth self. The end of the trunk could wake memories with the smallest smell, pressed to the Jacobson's organ in the roof of the mouth. The organ was a pathway into labyrinths of association. Memories arose the way they were called up by a smell in a human mind, but a hundred times more powerfully. Mammoth memories had solidity to them. They were roads one could walk, paths back to other times, into pasts as material and real as the present, conjured with a stroke of the trunk along the roof of the mouth. Hot grass scent—summer—sunshine—sunburn—a cot in a summer camp—blackberry-stained fingers—a boy's hands tangled in the hair at the nape of her neck. Skim of algae on the water—the boat dock at the village lake—the hollow clunk of one aluminum boat against another—oars in the hands—glide-drift—blisters in the web between thumb and forefinger.

Hands she did not have. A body she did not have. Memories from another life. A Damira she was not.

HER LAST MEMORY of her life before—the life that had been cut short half a century ago—was of sitting in that comfortable chair, in the white of the laboratory. She was drifting, a pleasant buzz in her, a hum distributed through her entire body. For the first time in a long time, she was not thinking of the war. She was simply here, among memories that were further away. Child times, student times. Vanillin of the old libraries guarding books no one had scanned and uploaded. The woodsmoke and frost of winters in Tomsk.

"How are you feeling?" the woman in the lab coat asked.

"Fine."

"Good. We are nearly done."

She glanced at her terminal, on the table. At the message floating on the lock screen:

Come quickly. Wamugunda is dead.

DAMIRA STROKED HER trunk along the hair at the base of her legs, where the smell of the blood-trail, of Koyon and Yekenat's agonies, still lingered. Turning, walking down the line of matriarchs, she touched it to each of their mouths in turn. They were getting tired.

She needed them alert. As she touched the death-scent to their faces, as she stroked it onto their flexible lips, she saw them startle. Saw the tiredness fade. They flapped their ears in anger. They tossed their heads in horror.

Good.

When she reached the end of the line, she turned and began to run, gaining speed. She did not trumpet, as she normally would have done. She ran as silently as an animal of her size could. She swung her tusks slightly side to side, in rhythm and counterbalance to the increasing speed of her strides, leaning forward, letting their weight pull her down the hill to her target.

The others followed, running now, keeping pace with her, their matriarch.

FOUR

THE CURTAINS WERE red velvet. The soft, overstuffed seats were upholstered in the same color. The walls were paneled in dark, polished walnut, reflecting the warm light of the gleaming brass sconces along them. The floor was parquet, softened with Azerbaijani, Turkmen, and Persian carpets. A reading lamp cast a soft circle of light on the table. A green leather-bound book lay on a white lace doily, the embossed gold letters on its cover catching in the light: *A Journey into Mammoth Country: Your Guide to the Ice Age World.*

The chamber had been built to evoke a train car—a luxury compartment from the old Trans-Siberian Express, perhaps. One could almost imagine sitting by the window, watching the endless Russian forests flow past in the night as the wash of rail-rhythm soothed the brain.

Almost. The cabin lurched and rocked like a ship in a storm. Strange groans and rattles emanated from behind the wood paneling. Engine moans welled up from under the Bukharan rugs and parquet floor. The chamber tilted. It rose and fell, more like a ship on a stormy sea than a train of any kind.

Vladimir came out of the toilet, steadying himself against the door frame, waiting for a pause in the motion of the cabin before crossing to one of the seats and throwing himself onto it. Behind him, the bathroom door hung open. It drew back and then slammed shut, rattling the amber glass of its illuminator.

Vladimir had washed his face and hands at the sink. He smelled of old-fashioned, scented floral soap and vomit. He smelled as if he had thrown up in someone's twee garden of lavender and roses.

"I don't see what the fuck the nineteenth century has to do with the Ice Age, anyway."

Anthony, his husband, looked at him from across the table.

"Don't look at me that way, Ant."

"I'm not looking at you in any *way*. I'm just *looking* at you."

"I'm trying. I am . . ."

"It's seasickness," said Anthony.

"Is that what it is?" Vladimir asked. "Not something I expected to encounter in the middle of the taiga."

"Not technically the taiga, here. We've been climbing for some time. We are about to reach the plateau."

"The who?"

"The plateau," Anthony said. "The mammoth steppe. The grassland that is the center of their preserve. You haven't been doing your homework, Dima."

Anthony parted the red curtains. With the lights on in their compartment, and no moon outside, there was little to see but his own face reflected back at him—but he caught, a bit behind them and off to the side, the lights of the two other Burlak trucks, bobbing in the darkness.

"Well," Vladimir said, "the preserve has some spectacularly terrible roads."

"There are no roads," answered Anthony. "That's why we need these beasts, with their low-pressure tires bigger than a man. These are some of the only vehicles that can travel overland out here."

"I bet you watched a dozen streams about them before we came out."

"A hundred, probably. They are amphibious as well, you know."

"They *feel* amphibious. They're making *me* feel amphibious."

Anthony looked at him again.

"I know that look. I know exactly what you are thinking," Vladimir said. "Land of my ancestors. I should be experiencing some sense of connection to this place. Some sort of tingly sensation at my return to my roots. I know. And I feel bad that

I don't. Because I want to. When we were walking around Red Square, I was almost forcing myself to feel something—some *frisson* of connection. But I don't. And why would I? That's magical thinking. I never saw this place, Ant. I was born in London. And my grandparents *fled* Moscow. They were driven out. What did the state label them? *Foreign Agents.* For what? For running a non-profit organization funded by some Western donors, trying to correct cleft lips and palates. I mean, Christ—correcting cleft palates. How are you going to overturn the state doing that? This place is insane. London hasn't even had an embassy here for what—twenty years now?"

"Twenty-five."

"A quarter of a century. More than half my life, Ant."

"I only wanted—"

"Listen." Vladimir took Anthony's hand across the table. "I'm fine. I know this means a lot to you. And it's really interesting. An adventure. And I know how much it all cost—"

"It's not the money."

"No, but it's an outrageous amount of money to toss away sulking and throwing up in the bathroom, and I want you to know—I'm not sulking. I just feel strange here. In Moscow, especially on the tour, I felt like everyone was looking at us as if we were aliens. Half of them glared at us like they hated us. And the other half looked terrified of us. As if even being near us was like breathing a poisonous gas. And I was reminded of my grandparents. That's one time I really did feel a connection. I bet that is exactly how they looked, before they managed to get out. Like these people. My grandfather wouldn't even *talk* about Russia. He would get up and leave the room if someone brought up the subject."

"It's brought up a lot of memories, coming here."

"Yes—but not *my* memories. I feel like it's brought up *their* memories. I felt, in Moscow, like I was disturbing a grave. It's better out here, at least."

"Why is that?"

"Because they were urban people. Muscovites who would

never have set foot in a place like this. When I was a stupid little kid with a bunch of fantasies about where I came from, my head filled with onion domes and church bells and sleigh rides through the cedars, I once asked my grandfather if he had seen a bear. Do you know what he said? He said, 'The only bears I ever saw wore expensive Savile Row tailored suits and ties that cost more than your life. But they were much deadlier than anything you would find in a forest.'"

"God, I wish I had met that man."

"I'm glad he's gone, Ant. He would have been furious with you for bringing me here. Absolutely furious."

The Burlak lurched to a stop. They were on level ground.

"I hear things might be getting better," said Anthony. "I hear the new president is a bit of a reformer."

From behind the parted curtains, Vladimir saw flashlights bobbing in the dark. Through the thickened glass he could hear men speaking in Russian. In the pool of the other Burlak's headlights the steppe grass was gray and metallic, as still as if it had been scratched into the surface of the earth with an etching needle.

Out there, somewhere, were mammoths. Real ones—wild, a part of this landscape again.

"Really?" Vladimir said. "You heard the new guy is a reformer? I heard a rumor that he *is* the old president. I heard they uploaded his mind before he went mad, and then downloaded it into a new body. A body the Russian government grew in a . . . in a vat, or something."

"That's the most ridiculous thing I've ever heard, Dima. Who do you *talk* to?"

"Where did this new president come from? Nobody had ever even heard of this man before. Then all of a sudden there he is, ruling one of the most powerful countries on earth."

Outside they were shifting the Burlaks into place, moving the other two until the three trucks were parked to form a Greek delta symbol. Circling the wagons. Anthony imagined flaming arrows arcing out of the darkness, and laughed.

"You laugh," Vladimir said, "but have you really looked at him? He looks like a wax mannequin out of Madame Tussauds. As if a mannequin got up and started walking around."

"They do, nowadays. But anyway, that's nonsense. And the old president looked like he was made of wax as well."

"Exactly!"

"Dima, every politician in the world looks like they are made of wax. You're being paranoid. Who have you been hanging around with while I am away on business?"

"Ant—there are *mammoths* out there in the darkness. *Mammoths* wandering around out there. And God knows what else. We live in a world where anything is possible."

They stopped, hearing footsteps on their Burlak's access ladder. Then the rear door to the cabin opened.

The man standing in the door wore a Norwegian hunting jacket and was bare-headed, although the night air that came in with him couldn't have been more than a few degrees above freezing.

"Good evening, gentlemen. I am Dr. Almas Aslanov. This is my national preserve. I am honored to have you here as my guests."

FIVE

DAMIRA COULD NOT forget the feeling of waking up. The horror of it. She woke unable to move, unable to speak, unable to open her eyes. It was like sleep paralysis, which she had experienced only twice in her life—once as a little girl in her bedroom in Tomsk, and once as a student in Saint Petersburg. But this was far worse. She was unable to even perceive the *location* of her eyes, her hands—any part of her body. Where was she? What had happened to her? *When* was she? Where was the light?

"Dr. Damira Khismatullina?"

The voice was no voice she recognized. She struggled to answer, to find the pathways to the muscles that would allow speech. To feel them, anywhere. They were nowhere.

"The connectome is online, but it has only been functioning for a few seconds now. There will be a good deal of confusion."

Another voice. But she wasn't *hearing* the voices. It was as if they were *registering* somehow in her mind, as if *written there*, without the sensation of hearing them. As if they just appeared in her consciousness. In this void that enclosed her—no, even enclosed was not correct. This void that *was* her.

I'm here, she thought.

"There she is," the second voice said. "She's responsive."

"Thank God," the first voice answered. "Damira, my name is Dr. Almas Aslanov. We can hear you—we can communicate. All you need to do to get through to us is to shape the words in your mind that way. To think them."

"Like this?" And she thought she heard a voice, somewhere in a room—like the echo of a voice speaking on a terminal, filled with interference.

"Yes. Like that. I know you must be very confused. And what I am going to tell you now is going to make it much worse. But we don't have much time, and I need you to decide. It will be one of the most important, and most difficult, decisions you have ever had to make. You will not be given much time to make it. You will be making it under terrible, terrible conditions. I will give you as much information as I can, and then leave you to make this decision. And whatever you decide, we will respect it. We cannot force you to do what we need you to do—we can only ask it of you. But I want to tell you now—many lives depend upon the choice you will make here, today. Do you understand all of that?"

"Where is here? What is today?"

"Those are good questions. Let me start at the beginning."

"You may not want to do that," the second voice said. "We've found it can be very . . . disruptive."

"I won't begin this relationship by lying to her. This part is hard, but there will be many things that are harder, ahead."

"I want to know," Damira said. Again, that voice—computer-modulated, drained of human emotion. "If something has happened to me, if I am paralyzed . . . whatever it is, I want to know."

"Yes," said Dr. Aslanov. "Everything I have read about you tells me that is exactly what you would want. You've lived a life of almost unbelievable courage, battling poachers and governments and international cartels to save the last of the wild elephants in Africa. Nobody fought like you did to save them."

"Plenty of people fought like I did to save them. Thousands of people fought like I did to save them." *Musa, Wamugunda . . .*

"What are those words?" Dr. Aslanov asked.

"Names, I think," the second voice answered.

There was no difference between thinking and speaking.

She heard that computer-modulated voice—her voice—say, "There is no difference between thinking and speaking." She continued. "Musa. Wamugunda. Those are just two names. My closest friends in Kenya. But there were so many others who fought as I did. I was just the only one who looked like you, and spoke Russian."

Come quickly. Wamugunda is dead.

Panic rose in her. But it was strange—there was no *feeling* of panic—no bodily feeling—instead there was just a sudden scattering of her thoughts, as if a wave had crashed through them. "You need to tell me what has happened to me."

"Dr. Damira Khismatullina, you were murdered."

"Injured, you mean. I'm in a hospital."

"No. You were *murdered*. You were killed by a group of poachers. Your camp was attacked. There were seven of you there. They shot the others, but you—they wanted to make an example of you. You were hacked to death with machetes. They delivered your head to the president as a warning to stop fighting them. He did not stop fighting them. He tried, instead, to use your death as a rallying cry. He tried to make you a martyr. He went to the UN and gave a speech that made you a saint, a symbol of the fight. But he did not outlive you by long. He was assassinated six months later."

"How can this be? I was just in Moscow. I hadn't returned yet, I . . ."

"Your memories—the memories of this version of you—would end here, in Moscow, on the day of your uploading."

"None of this makes sense." Again, panic—not as a bodily feeling, but as the scattering of thought, the confusion of reasoning. As if a boulder had been dropped into water.

"I know. But I need you to think. You will come to understand this is true. What is the last thing you remember?"

Come quickly. Wamugunda is dead.

"I received a message on my terminal. A message that my friend had been killed. And then . . . I remember . . . I tried to stand up. The technician asked me to sit down. She told me we were almost done. Thirty seconds. I could barely sit still. Then she came around the counter, and . . . that's it. It's the last thing I remember."

"Yes. That uploading of your connectome to storage occurred a little less than a year before your murder."

"But how long have you waited to bring me back? You said the president was assassinated six months *after* I was killed."

"Yes. And all of that happened over a century ago. Doctor, we are seeking to bring you back because you are a most extraordinary person. Not only were you the leading expert in elephant behavior of your time . . . you are also the only existing human mind that remembers elephants in the wild. The only mind that knew them. We still have elephants in zoos—the ones we have been able to protect from poaching—and in research facilities—but those are captive elephants, raised by humans. They are not the same."

"We failed. I failed."

"You did everything you could. You sacrificed your life. But yes—we failed. Humanity failed. The African elephant was driven into extinction in the wild a decade or so after your death. The Asian elephant outlived its African cousin by a few years. Soon enough, armed men were attacking zoos to get at the last of the elephants. The ones that are left now are in heavily guarded facilities. I know it must be a shock, knowing they are gone."

"No. I knew it would happen. I knew we could not stop it. I saw it happening. Nothing could stop the greed that was destroying them." But as she said these words, she knew they were not true. She had thought that, somehow, they would win. She had always believed that. And now it must have been grief that made the words of her thoughts seem to splinter in her mind, falling to pieces as she fought to keep their syllables composed.

"You knew, but you kept fighting."

"What else could we do?"

"And that is why we need you, Doctor."

"You need me?" And it felt strange to say it, but there were no other words for it: "What more could you possibly need from me? I am dead."

"I need you to help save my mammoths. We have done all we can. We stitched as much of their genetic code back together as we could, we spliced and reconstructed what we could recover— all of the differences between their DNA and elephant DNA, all of the changes made in their genes over the nearly six million years since they diverged from the Asian elephant. We sequenced it fragment by fragment, using the broken strands of DNA recovered from mummified specimens, and once we had completed that massive puzzle, we used surrogate Asian elephants to give birth to the first calves. This was all accomplished even before I joined the project. Much of the hardest work was done even before my birth. But the sequencing, and the births in captivity, were only the first of so many steps. We didn't want mammoths in the zoo, to be gawked at. We wanted the mammoth in its own habitat. And not an individual—a species. We cleared land for them, created an entire national preserve centered on the last of the mammoth steppe—a place where they could roam free, re-establish a species, and re-establish, perhaps, a lost ecosystem."

"You should have brought back my elephants instead."

"Yes," Dr. Aslanov said. "I understand that point of view. I do. But there would be nowhere to *put* your elephants if they were brought back. Their world is still unsafe. But in Siberia, we have given the mammoth a place to thrive. A chance at a new life for an entire species. And if we can solve this puzzle of de-extinction—really solve it—then maybe one day we will be able to bring your elephants back to their savannahs as well. We are so close to solving the problem: we have a sufficiently diverse population, now, of mammoths. We raised not one but dozens of them in captivity. We used several variants of DNA. And we have a place for them to live, protected. To roam free. It is a life's work. Several lives'. But once we released them, they began to die. They wandered, confused. They failed to form proper groups.

They hurt themselves needlessly. We've lost thirteen of them in three seasons, and there have been no births in the wild."

"Why? What went wrong?"

"I said before that you are the only existing human mind that worked and lived with wild elephants. And that is true. But I should have put it another way. You are the only existing mind *of any kind* that knows the culture of elephants. The last wild elephant died over half a century ago. Our surrogates were raised in captivity, as was every elephant they know. Wild elephant culture is dead on planet Earth, except in one place: your mind. And wild elephant culture is the closest we'll ever get to wild mammoth culture, which disappeared when the last mammoths died out eight thousand years ago."

"Mammoths didn't *die out*. They were driven to extinction by humans. Just like practically every other extant species of megafauna."

"Many theories say it was simply the warming of the planet, the change in their ecosystem."

"Their species had survived every other warm interval. They had always declined, hidden in refugial habitats. It wasn't until this time around that they disappeared entirely. Why? We all know why. The difference this time was us. We killed them. And the beavers as big as bears, and the North American horse, and the North American camel. And the ground sloth. And the short-faced bear. And the moa. I could go on . . ."

Anger, too, she felt like a scattering of her thoughts. It was a confusion of their order, of their weight. A shivering through her mind that threatened to splinter logic.

"You are probably right."

"I *am* right."

"But now is our chance to bring them back. Giants will walk the earth again—and you will be a part of that."

"Giants may walk the earth again, but for how long? The problem you are trying to solve—how to bring animals back from extinction—it's the wrong problem. Extinction has only one cause, and that cause is older, even, than the wheel. That cause is human greed."

She heard the echo of her own voice. A digital rasp in that room—the room where Dr. Aslanov was standing.

A room in the real world. A room of flesh and blood. A space, a physical space. It would feel so good to move in the world again—to feel the connective tissues of a body. To stand, to lift an arm. To see. To be alive again.

"Tell me what you propose. What you want from me."

"We propose to make you a matriarch. We propose to transfer your mind into one of theirs. You will lead them. You will teach them how to *be* mammoths. Under your leadership, they will thrive."

SHE CRASHED INTO the tent, lifting her forelegs and bringing them down again and again, twisting from side to side, stomping. She could feel them—the bodies giving way under her enormity, the shattering of them, the bursting of the weak little bags that contained what they were. The crying out of the tiny, fragile men.

She moved away and the others rushed in. The tent was a loose sack now, poles down. Kara raised her legs and brought them down repeatedly. She tangled the tent in her tusks and dragged it. Then another mammoth strode across it. Turned, trampled it again. And another, and another—until the tent was nothing but a mangled stain—more a pool than a heap, nearly as flat as the land around it.

They found the mule-things and knocked them to the ground, dragged them, stepped on them, feeling their joints give way and snap, driving them into the soil.

Kara stood by the last of the mule-things. She stroked the end of her trunk over the tusks strapped to it. Koyon's tusks, Yekenat's tusks. She nudged them and the mule-thing tipped over. Another mammoth, Temene, moved next to Kara. Temene touched the tusks as well, put her trunk in her mouth, and then stroked the side of Kara's face with the end of her trunk, rumbling.

Then others came, until Kara was surrounded. Their trunks stroked her sides and face, her ears. They touched her with their feet. The calves reached out to her, tugging at her hair, touching her face with the pink ends of their trunks. The rumble moved back and forth between them all. Damira could feel it, vibrating up from the ground through her bones. The group sound, both in the air and in the ground. Seismic waves that traveled from her toenails, conducted by her bones, to her ear, so that she did not only hear the sound of them, together—she felt it move through her, vibrating in her blood and bone.

The together feeling. She moved into the circle as well. It parted to accommodate her, accepted her, enlarged and remade itself with her inclusion. She raised her trunk and stroked Kara's face, tasting her grief with the others.

When she turned to leave, they all followed. Kara trailed behind a bit, smelling Koyon, conjuring him from his remains. Just for a moment—but even she was eager to be gone from that place, which stank now of death. Of the burst, mangled bodies of men and the stench they carried inside them.

SIX

IT WAS TOO cold to keep hiding. Svyatoslav could not remain still anymore. With the plastidown blanket wrapped around him, he crept down the hill.

He had been sleeping on a small rise, about a hundred meters from the camp, when the attack came. He'd chosen that spot because the ground there was flat, and dry. He had drifted off looking at the stars. They were so dense here, in this landscape without light, with no moon to dull them, that he could imagine trade routes between them, civilizations weaving a web of ships. He remembered an ancient map he had once seen, of trade routes across the Mediterranean. The map depicted some of the features of the shore, but mostly it showed the main trading ports, with distanced-marked lines connecting them to one another. Not a map of terrain, or of the sea itself—a map of connectivity. That was what he saw in the stars above him as well. With enough societies, with enough energy, with enough technology, you could build a web of life that stretched over even those distances.

This was how his mind moved, when he was alone. These were his private thoughts, told to no one. To his father, the drone Svyatoslav piloted was a toy. To Svyatoslav, it was part of much more. With it, he reached out beyond the confines of his body. He looked from another position down on his world. Saw himself and others for what they were—miniscule, embedded in a much larger world, a world which itself was just a point in something vast.

To his father, Siberia *was* the world, and it was enough. This land was big enough for anything, and he knew it the way few others knew it. He never thought of leaving it: he thought of mastering it, taking from it, using it. But for Svyatoslav this vastness was just a point, a peripheral node in a network of connections. Mastering technology could bring him to other places. Skills were rays pointing outward. They became line segments when you discovered where they led. To other points. To a university in another country, maybe. And that university would be a point more central to the network—a point from where he would be able to view many segments, many connections. He would be able to see, then, his place in this network of possibilities. He would be able to move in it. To move away from all of this, out into a wider world.

His mother had been a geography teacher in a secondary school. She had brought maps home since before he could remember, showing him a world that was both limitless and accessible: if it could be documented, it was real. It could be *reached*.

One of his first memories was of a map. He remembered sitting on his mother's lap, at the table in their little kitchen. It was night, and snowing outside the window. He could see the flakes when they came close to the window or when a gust of wind whirled them against the glass. He could see the snow as it fell into the haloes of the streetlamps, solar systems whirling in the darkness. His mother's arm was around him. She sang softly under her breath. On the table was a notebook, a blue pen, and a book. The book was open to a map. She stopped taking notes and pointed to a place on the map. An island off the boot of Italy.

"This is called Sicily. We could go there one day." She moved her finger. "Or we could go here. This island is called Corsica."

"Corsica."

"That's right."

"How do we get there?"

"On a train, and then a plane, and maybe then a ship. There are many ways."

"When will we go?"

"It's up to us."

He was afraid to lose this memory. He returned to it often, like a person checking their pockets to make sure their keys were still there. He had already lost so many memories of her. The further away he moved from the day of her death, the more she faded. So he had named this memory "Corsica" to give it a place in his mind. And he had given names to other memories of her, often associated with maps or with her talking about maps. He had memories of her named Astrakhan, Colchis, Wakhan, Gondwanaland, Ashgabat, Cyclades, Alkebulan, Thebes . . .

But he knew there were so many other memories lost. You could only remember what stood out, what was different. But most days lacked reference points. They were like the surface of water—undifferentiated, too mobile for the eye to rest upon. He'd forgotten almost everything already, and the face he remembered was nothing like her face had really been. The details were slipping away.

He woke to a vibration. Then he heard a man scream. He did not stand up—instinct kept him pinned to the grass. He crawled to a place where he could see the camp.

The shapes of the mammoths in the moonless dark were like holes torn in the sky—gaps where stars were missing. He saw the tent, mashed flat against the ground. One of the mammoths dragged it with its tusks. If anything still moved inside that crushed sack, he could not see it. Another mammoth walked across it, turned in a circle, mashing it further into the earth.

If Svyatoslav had ever been afraid before, it was nothing like this. This was the full weight of fear, pressing him into the earth. Pressing him so hard he felt he would sink beneath the soil forever.

Into the frozen underworld with Nga.

Something moaned from inside the crushed tent. He heard the mammoths' feet coming down, heard sounds like tree branches breaking. He knew what the sounds were. He covered his head with his hands, his face pressed into the grass. He was silent, but still afraid the mammoths would be able to hear his heart beating, the rush of blood through his body. He heard them going for the drone mules, heard the sounds of metal twisting, joints snapping. Then the sounds of the mammoths themselves. Of the mammoths *talking* to one another. A rumble that came through the air but also up through the earth, through his blood and bone.

He lay a long time like that, after he knew they were gone. Even after he was certain they had left, no mental effort would unlock his joints and force them to move again. He must have been there for an hour before a night frost settled on him and he started to shiver.

It was the shivering that finally freed him, allowed him to move a hand, a finger, then the rest of his body. He wrapped the plastidown blanket around himself, got to his feet, and went down the hill.

With movement came thought. They were dead, but he was not. He had to gather things. He had to gather food from their stores, the shelter of the emergency tent, his sleeping bag. He had to find his way out of this place. It would be days of travel. He had to do it without the mammoths finding him. These thoughts drove death out of his head—the death of the men, of his father—even the possibility of his own death.

He was free.

The thought took him completely by surprise. It did not seem to come from inside him—it came down from the stars.

Free. When he walked out of this place, he would have nothing at all. No father, no mother, no home—not even a name, if he did not want it. Everything was destroyed. All of it. And that meant anything was possible now. All he had to do was survive this, move on from here.

He caught the death-smell of blood and feces, wafting from the mutilated tent, hammered flat and leaking gore onto the landscape. It knocked him to his knees.

Dead. His father. The others. Butchered.

"Get up, boy."

He turned his head. He expected to see his father there, standing against the stars with that smirk of his on his face. And maybe then he would wake up from this.

It was Myusena. Behind him, Svyatoslav could see his tracks through the grass—dark holes in the thin layer of frost that had settled on the camp.

"Get up. We have a lot to do. We need to collect food, any weapons that survived. I need to see if any of the mules can be repaired, so we can get those tusks out of here and not have to carry them ourselves . . ."

Svyatoslav had forgotten about the tusks.

"This land does not wait for people to mourn. It simply carries them off to join the dead. I need you to move. The mammoths may return."

The tent . . . the tent was steaming in the cold. Releasing the heat of the dead men inside.

"We need to help them. Maybe one of them is still . . ."

"No. None of them are alive, boy. And if one of them were, he would not be for long. But I need to get in there, and see what can be salvaged." Myusena drew a knife from his belt, and started to the tent. He looked like a man about to gut a deer, nothing more. "You go and see if you can get that mule with the tusks on it upright. I think it's less damaged than the rest. I'll take care of this."

"But how did you get away?"

"A *sihirtia* dug his way up from underground and woke me from my slumber. He told me to run into the darkness."

Svyatoslav stared at him blankly.

"I'm kidding, kid. I just took the luckiest shit of my life."

SEVEN

"I DON'T UNDERSTAND," Vladimir said. "It's your preserve. They are your mammoths. Why not just use their GPS trackers to find them? It would be easier than all of this searching."

Dr. Aslanov had just taken a bite of scrambled eggs. He shook his head as he finished chewing. "They don't have GPS trackers."

"How can that be possible? You mean *you don't know where your mammoths are?*"

Dr. Aslanov shook his head. "No, we don't. And for good reason. Humankind learned hard lessons from the extinction of the African and Asian elephants. One of them was about digital information: if *you* can access something, so can the poachers. The cartels catch up with every encryption you can invent. They break into every system you can design. In Botswana, where the last of the African elephants lived in the wild, the rangers could not understand how the poachers were finding them. Then they discovered the cartels backing the poachers had not only penetrated the GPS system—they had also broken into their drone feeds, the encrypted communications of the rangers, the UN satellite mapping the movements of the last herds, the communications of every NGO working on elephant preservation. The cartels used the system against itself. All that technology scientists had designed to help them save the elephants ultimately doomed them. And the rangers, in the end—undersupplied, overworked—the ones who did not die for their cause . . . gave it up. The last of them threw their rifles down, and melted away. We won't have that here. What protects us is the vastness of this place. Its remoteness. In order to even penetrate the preserve, you have to cross hundreds of miles of taiga and steppe. There are no roads—we tore out the few roads that had been here."

"And no rangers?"

"There are rangers—a few. They patrol on horseback. But most of the preserve's security is conducted the old way—the Tsarist way."

"I don't get that," Anthony said. He was sitting on his folding camp stool, wearing a waxed canvas jacket, wolfing down eggs. He looked comfortable, in his element.

Vladimir was not. With every forkful of eggs, he still felt the roll of the Burlak's cabin, and his stomach fought to keep his breakfast down.

But it was beautiful here. The dawn light was citrine, the sun's sudden heat turning the frost into a haze over the undulating plateau. "Yes—I don't get that, either. The Tsarist way. What does that mean?"

"Spies. Informants. We pay the locals in the villages and towns for information. For rumors. Anybody talking about entering the preserve. Anyone they see passing through who shouldn't be there. We pay them well—well enough that if any of *them* decided to lead an expedition into this place, we would know about it right away. One of their own family members would turn them in, or someone who overheard them in a café."

"And that works?" asked Vladimir.

"The old methods work best. The informant system is as foolproof as anything technology can come up with. Listen—there are two Russian proverbs you should know." Dr. Aslanov held up his hand, and counted them off on thumb and index finger. "One: 'The sober man's secret is the drunkard's speech.' Two: 'Confide a secret to a mute man, and he will speak.' They are more than proverbs: they are truths. Between the two of these truths, the system of informants is as close to foolproof as you can get. But the informants are only half the system. The other half is disinformation. We spread rumors: terrible technologies that wait for the poachers. Land mines triggered by human pheromones.

DNA-seeking bullets. Suicide drones the size of a bumblebee that will blow your head into a red mist. And one of my favorites: robotic cave lions that can run as fast as a high-speed train. If it inspires terror, we invent it. This was the other side of the Tsar's coin—not just the collection of information, but the dispersal of disinformation. The two of them working together form a simple, efficient method of control."

"I seem to remember the last Tsar ended up machine-gunned in a basement with the rest of his family," Anthony said.

Dr. Aslanov shrugged. "In the end, all systems collapse. But I hope long before that happens here we will see mammoths roaming a steppe that stretches from the Pacific to the Atlantic. Their return means the return not just of some wooly elephants— it is the return of an entire ecosystem. Their browsing pushes back the forest and encourages the steppe grasses to grow. In the winter, their pushing away of the snow in search of grasses underneath exposes the soil to frigid air, protecting the permafrost. The mammoths are building a more resilient world. They are helping us to undo at least some of the damage man has done."

"And you are bringing people in to shoot them," Vladimir said.

One of the guides brought another panful of scrambled eggs. Vladimir found that his appetite was returning, now. And he was hungrier than he had expected. Maybe it was the altitude.

"Yes."

"After all of this investment in keeping people from shooting them."

"Yes."

"If he's getting under your skin," Anthony said, "I'm sorry. But that's just what he does. There's nothing to be done about it. If you try to put a stop to it, it just makes it worse."

"It is fine," Dr. Aslanov said. "It is the way my colleagues and I all speak to one another. All we do is argue. I'm not sure we would be able to have a conversation without arguing. We joke that for us de-extinctionists, arguing really *is* the scientific method."

Vladimir had finished chewing his eggs. "If you're trying to avoid my questions—both of you—I haven't forgotten."

"He never forgets," Anthony said. "Trust me. He'll just keep at you until you answer."

"I don't mind answering. It is a good question. We keep the poachers at bay because they would quickly wipe out the population we have built here. There are only a few hundred mammoths now. Ivory has disappeared from the wild. In Asia and Africa, even the feet and skin of the elephants became commodities, dooming the few elephants without tusks to the fate of the others. In the Arctic, the business of extracting mammoth tusks from the permafrost was eventually outlawed—the environmental degradation was too great. The tusk hunters were spraying the riverbanks with high-pressure hoses, filling the water with silt. There were gangs of them in the thousands after the price of ivory went up. Even outlawed, that practice still continues. If those kinds of people began to get in here, the ivory wars would begin again."

"Not an answer," Vladimir said.

"No. Background. The answer is the same as always. The answer is money. The government demands the preserve become self-sustaining. That means revenue. The mammoth has no predators, yet—we have not brought back the steppe wolf, the cave lion, the massive Ice Age bears that might have been able to prey on their calves. The mammoths share their range only with caribou and bison, while we work on bringing back the wooly rhinoceros to keep them company. So there is room—limited, controlled room—for the hunting of a few of the males."

"I can't see how that could possibly be worth it," Vladimir said.

"Then I take it Anthony has not told you just how much he has paid for the privilege."

Vladimir looked at Anthony, in his waxed shooting jacket, scraping up the last of his eggs with his fork.

"How much?"

"There was a secret auction, Dima. Several of us bid for the privilege."

"How much?"

"Enough to keep this preserve operational for a long time," Dr. Aslanov said. "Enough to help us continue to protect the mammoth here until after my retirement."

"How much is that?"

Anthony shrugged. "It was somewhere around a year of my income."

"Good God. That's—"

Anthony interrupted. "Please spare us the comparisons with the GDP of small countries, et cetera."

The breakfast table, with its white tablecloth clamped to its metal aluminum frame, was set up just outside the triangle formed by the three Burlaks. Its view extended across kilometers of plateau, toward a range of mountains that could have been very far off, and extraordinarily high, or low and much closer. The plateau was nearly orange now in the light, and a dusting of snow on the mountains reflected a pale pink.

Now that the question had moved to the hunt itself, to the why of it, Vladimir had been arguing with only half his attention. And he knew Anthony. Many people had a part of themselves they kept from others—some dark place they went to, into which they did not let strangers, friends, or kin. Anthony's was larger than most, and hunting was at the core of it.

If Vladimir wanted, he could start another argument about it—about what he had called, during other fights, Anthony's need to perform "ritual murder." About the hypocrisy of cloaking that need in some idea about conservation. But the argument never went anywhere: Vladimir would accuse Anthony of bloodthirstiness, of cruelty, of atavistic, backward tendencies. You think you're Hemingway, he would say. You think you're the Great White Hunter. You think you're Teddy Roosevelt. But you aren't. You are just a spectacularly rich man who gets his kicks killing animals.

But that wasn't it. Vladimir had seen the pictures, which Anthony showed to no one else, of him with the animals he killed.

He was never happy in those pictures. Never smiling. He looked like he had done exactly what Vladimir accused him of. He looked like he had committed murder. Worse, he looked like he had killed something he loved. In every hunting photo, Anthony looked hollowed out. Drained.

Anthony kept no trophies of the animals he killed. He allowed no pictures of him not taken on his own encrypted terminal. There was no Bluebeard room filled with taxidermized prizes at their elegant country estate. There was nothing at all, no record of the destruction, except that slideshow of devastating photos. Over and over again, in variations, the same image: an exhausted, defeated man. A dead animal lying where it had fallen. Both looked as if they had lost everything that meant anything to them.

Vladimir had never traveled with Anthony before on any of these expeditions. He had not been asked to, and if he had been asked, he would have refused. But this time, Anthony had invited him, and although he had expected to turn it down, he found himself saying yes. Why?

To understand, perhaps. To see the moment, the act. To get a little closer to this man he loved, but did not know well.

Anthony and Dr. Aslanov were talking technical details: distances the Burlaks could travel, the part of the journey they would take on foot. Vladimir, meanwhile, was watching a man on horseback. He had appeared from behind a fold in the undulating landscape, and was growing larger as he made his way toward them. Again, the distances here were impossible for Vladimir to judge. Suddenly the man was almost upon them, and Vladimir could make out details: a dirty, padded camouflage jacket. The horse's glossy eye, the man's sunburned mask of a face. A few dozen meters away, he dismounted. The horse began cropping grass, and the man walked up to the table and said something to Dr. Aslanov in Russian. Or in what Vladimir thought was probably Russian. Again he was amazed by the idea that people related to him had spoken this language, which he found completely impenetrable. That people who carried his genetic code had been able to decipher this series of sounds, and had lived inside its cadences.

"This is Konstantin—my head ranger. He says they have found one. A male mammoth."

Anthony looked up.

The expression on Anthony's face was so startling Vladimir took a step back.

"How close?" Anthony asked.

Konstantin shrugged, and said in English, "A day, two. It depends how far he moves from us, depends on the terrain. But close."

Vladimir could not take his eyes off of Anthony's face in the morning sun.

He had never seen Anthony so happy.

EIGHT

THERE WAS NO way that Myusena would let him live. Svyatoslav understood that by the end of their first day alone together.

They had managed to get the mule upright with its load of tusks. The damage to it was minimal—as if the mammoths had not wanted to disturb the tusks, and so had spared this one. The other mules were crushed and mangled beyond repair, but Myusena had stripped them for parts, and collected what he salvaged in a bag he strapped to the one that was preserved. He had also gathered rations—mostly just compressed energy cakes, many crushed. The rice bags had been burst, the rice scattered. Much of the equipment that had been in the tent, Svyatoslav understood, was destroyed. But there was an emergency tent still strapped to the mules that had survived. Beyond that, they had the plastidown blanket Svyatoslav had taken with him, and Myusena's sleeping bag, retrieved from the tent. The sleeping bag was punctured and stained with blood, but salvageable. A backpack holding Svyatoslav's clothes, which had been strapped to one of the mules, was intact except for a tear in the bottom. They had managed to retrieve a few other tools intact from the tent: an axe, a few multitools. Of the rifles, only one was left unbroken—the old .375 Ruger M77 that had belonged to Svyatoslav's father.

They spent much of the morning gathering the supplies, stripping the mules, and loading up. Svyatoslav tried not to look at the tent. The trampled, bloodstained sack like some great, downed animal, mangled beyond recognition.

A mass grave, now. A collective shroud. They thought of burning it, but there was not enough fuel to be found here to get

THE TUSKS OF EXTINCTION   •   47

it alight. They might have buried it, but both collapsible shovels were bent beyond use.

In the end, they just walked away, with Myusena in the lead, carrying the rifle, and Svyatoslav trailing behind the mule, with its load of curving ivory and their salvaged supplies. The steppe here rolled off in a nearly featureless plain, punctuated here and there by a kurgan, or a depression through which a narrow stream flowed. In the distance were mountains, blue in the morning and then gray-brown in the afternoon, streaked here and there by snow. By noon it was hot, and difficult to imagine that frost had covered the ground the night before, or that in the winter everything would be smothered under meters of snow.

"How do they eat? In the winter?"

Svyatoslav had caught up to Myusena as they were fording a muddy rivulet, where swamp sucked at their boots.

"The same way the bison eat, or the reindeer, I suppose. They push away the snow and find the grass underneath. Don't you know these things?"

"We don't hunt in the winter."

We. Now, for the first time since that morning, he thought of his father. His dead father. There was no *we* anymore. He didn't feel anything—nothing like sadness, or grief. Nothing like he had felt when his mother had died. But one of his knees almost buckled, and Myusena steadied him. His grip was a clamp, without mercy. The sudden pain of it brought Svyatoslav back to the *now*—the sun on the back of his neck, the hum of mosquitoes, the suck of mud at his boots.

"I forgot," Myusena said. "You Russians just hide in the winter. Like bears, huddled in your apartment caves. Drinking, telling stories, smoking cigarettes. You stay in your cities and hope the power and the heat stay on. And if one day they don't . . ."

"Aren't you half-Russian?"

Myusena turned and looked him in the face.

That was when Svyatoslav knew it. Myusena would kill him.

He would not have been able to tell how he knew—but he was certain. He saw that Myusena had decided it, and that it would mean nothing to him at all.

"I say 'you' to whoever I want. When I talk to a Nenets I say, 'You just stay up here with your reindeer herds, pretending the world hasn't changed, banging on your shaman drums and fearing *Madna* and *Hansosyada*. You don't know fuck-all about the real world.' And when I come down among you Russians I say, 'All you can do is ruin things. You would take a shit in the only spring you have to drink from. You sit in the middle of the world's richest forest—a forest that stretches forever—in your concrete boxes, playing *durak* with a greasy deck of cards all winter and eating tinned meat.'"

The mule got a foot stuck in the mud, and Myusena yanked it out and shoved the drone up the incline.

"You don't get to tell me who I am, boy. I say 'you' to whoever I want, and nobody tells me I am half this, half that. Do you know what my name means? Nomad. Born on the move. *I* decide where I stand. *I* decide where I go, and why."

"I apologize. I didn't mean anything by it," Svyatoslav said.

"Nobody means anything."

A few hours later they stopped to eat—compressed energy cakes, but it was an opportunity to sit down, at least. They were walking in the right direction: Svyatoslav had memorized the face of one of the mountains, with a landslide on it like a wound. When they had come into the preserve, they had come through a low pass out of a larch forest, and put that mountain at their backs. But they had been in the preserve for days after that. How far away was it?

"They say here in the preserve they have an autorifle that fires a bullet that can tune itself to a man's DNA. Like a little rocket that can sniff him out and kill him twenty kilometers away."

"They say a lot of things." Myusena was on his back, his eyes closed. "You should learn to look with your eyes, not with rumors."

"What do you mean?"

Myusena sat up. "You seen any drones in the sky? Since we've been here?"

"No."

"But in every dirty little hole of a restaurant, they were talking about drones. A thousand miles from here, every kid kicking a ragged football in the street knows—suicide drones thick as mosquitoes, DNA-tuned smart bullets . . ."

"They must protect the mammoths with something."

"I just told you what they protect them with. You don't listen."

They walked endlessly, their progress impeded by wet ground and mud, until the day began to fail. In the evening light, shadows shuddered where the wind hit the grass. Could it be that late, already? How much farther had they walked after lunch? Another five kilometers? Ten? Sometimes Myusena drew so far ahead of Svyatoslav that he was just a smudge, but the mule kept pace with Svyatoslav, or Svyatoslav kept pace with the mule—he wasn't sure which was the case. And Myusena wouldn't go anywhere without the mule.

He'd never called Dmitriy "papa"—never even thought it in his mind. And his mother had never said anything like "your papa"—something a mother would usually say. It was always "your father": "Your father is coming home today." "Your father is out with his friends."

My father is dead.

He caught up with Myusena as the sun was setting.

"We'll put the tent up here."

There was a depression, a muddy hole in which a dead tree stood, a circle of packed earth.

"We'll have a fire," Myusena said. "We can burn that dead tree for fuel. I managed to save a few bags of dehydrated soup. We need a hot meal. You did well, you know—after what happened. Get the tent set up."

"Have you ever heard of mammoths doing that . . . attacking people like that? It was like they hunted us."

"Mammoths are extinct, boy. Nobody knows anything about what they might have done when they were around. And these things are not mammoths: they are just some kind of copy. I think they just stumbled across us in the dark, and got scared."

"It didn't seem like that," Svyatoslav said. He glanced at the mule, standing near the dead, bleached tree with its load of ivory, which was stained where it had been hacked out of the mammoth bulls' faces.

Myusena followed his gaze.

"I keep reaching for my terminal," Myusena said. "Keep wanting to open up Kommodifi, see what the market price is. I keep forgetting I don't have it here. Addictive, those things."

"Markets?"

"Terminals. But yeah. Markets, too, I guess."

Svyatoslav's eyes wandered to the horizon. All day he had found himself staring at hummocks, kurgans, thinking they had shifted—lumbered out of place.

"Look—they're not tigers," Myusena said, as if reading his thoughts. "They're not stalking us, hiding in the grass. These things are big, and slow, and easy enough to hunt. They are prey, not predators. There's a reason they are extinct."

The mule shifted its weight, like a living thing. Its burden of curving ivory glowed in the evening light. Dim, warm, like a lamp behind a curtain. Was it beautiful? Beautiful enough for the price it would fetch on the market?

Yes, there was a reason mammoths were extinct.

NINE

THE SMELL OF FIRE.

As a mammoth, Damira had discovered a world of memory the human Damira never had. When she was human, memories were sometimes awakened by scent—but those memories were often nothing more than a feeling, or a flash of something, a fragment of a past event, dim and half-present.

She had once seen a bull elephant touch a bolus of dung left by another elephant with the tip of his trunk and bring the smell of it into his mouth to taste. Then he stood there, his eyes closed, a low vibration issuing from him into the earth. Remembering.

And now, as a mammoth, she knew what that meant. For an elephant, smells did not conjure feelings, fragments of scenes. No—they brought memories back whole, as material as glass beads on a string. One memory chained to another, and another, and another. Memories as complete and rich as the world of now.

The smell of fire. She remembered her first mammoth seasons—leading Kara and the others away from a brush fire. Nudging them into line. Teaching them to move away from the smoke smell, ford streams to find safe pasture.

Later in that first, brutal winter she had thought they would not make it—any of them. They had moaned and wandered, confused and half-starved, not understanding yet that they were *built* for this place, that their bodies were *expecting* it, that their genes had come *home* to here. They were still thinking like captive elephants, with the shattered culture of their elephant foster mothers, themselves raised in captivity, and the squalid, constrained mentality of the enclosure.

She broke those habits. She showed them how to clear snow from the grass and tear it out. She taught them that, although the world looked empty, there was sustenance—as much as in the summer, if you knew where to look for it. She taught them not to fear the cold and the snow. She knew their hemoglobin made red blood cells that excelled at moving oxygen through their massive bodies in the winter. That their hair would keep them insulated, that their metabolisms were designed for this environment. To think like the mammoths was to survive. To know this was not some alien world. This was *their* place, and they had come home to it.

Some of the skills she taught them were elephant skills, skills she had observed in the wild over her years among the elephants— her human years. She now tended the wild births in the warm season, taught her herd to form a square around the calves when they were under threat—although until the poachers came, there had been no real threats to them here. There had been no predator, in this world, that could bring a mammoth down.

Some of the skills she had learned from the elephants, and some of the skills she taught them were learned from books she had read about mammoths. Learned knowledge and book knowledge—she put both to use, and led.

The smell of fire.

The chain of memories wound back, past the mammoth years. Back, into Damira-as-human. And it was strange that now, in this body, she had access to those human memories in a way she never had when she lived in human form. She traveled *back there*. She was present, again, in her own past. She was present in the elephant way, inhabiting a past as real as this moment—as physical, as complete. All of that neural circuitry had been there, in her human mind, but human recall was inferior: it skirted along the pathways and brought their contents up garbled, fragmentary. It mixed things up, moved too easily from one loop of association along a branch into another. It was fallible and partial.

Not now. Mammoth memory was transportation to the past. The smell of fire, and she was there again . . .

WAMUGUNDA SAT IN front of the small fire they had made. The air had grown cool with the sunset. He had seen Damira shivering, and then gathered wood. She had wanted to protest—but they had no tent with them, no sleeping bags, no shelter but the Land Rover.

Their Land Rover had broken down while they were driving a transect in search of a herd. Here, the elephants were not tagged: they roamed free and unmonitored. The rangers did not trust the tags and drones still being used in the other parks. Tagged elephants, they said, were found by the poachers first. Herds sighted by monitor drones were attacked. So here, they found the elephants the old way—they went out and looked for them.

The biologists and rangers tracked the elephants by finding fresh dung, the raw wood of branches they had broken and stripped, the depressions of their padded feet at the watering holes. It was safer. But when their front axle broke, Wamugunda and Damira found that the car's electrical had failed as well, including the fuse for the charging station. Their terminals were dead.

They were alone, and it would be a long walk back to the camp the next day. But there was enough food and water, and they knew the way—so they were not worried. Their pleasure in studying and watching the elephants had already been scarred by the poachers' incursions into the park but it was not yet the worst of times, when the rangers and the biologists themselves would be targeted. The price of ivory was spiraling out of control, but the ivory wars that had already wiped out populations in Sudan, South Africa, and the Congo had not yet come here.

There was still some degree of innocence, which turned this mishap on a routine transect into an adventure. An unplanned camping trip; a welcome diversion from their mounting problems.

Wamugunda was telling her about his days as a student in

Hong Kong. On scholarship, on an island, studying species preservation in the most densely human-populated place on earth.

"Nowhere," Wamugunda said, "could there have been a world
that was more human, more urban, more different from rural life
here."

Wamugunda's father and grandfather had both been rangers
in the park. He had never been an urban Kenyan, and before his
student days, had never even traveled to Nairobi.

"My urban metaphor was termite mounds. That was what
Hong Kong seemed like to me—towers like termite warrens, of
steel and glass instead of red earth. You always looked at people
from above, or saw them in crowds that made them faceless. Too
many people, and they become identical.

"I grew up here, where you learn every animal and person by
name—their qualities, their capacities, where they fit in. You
learn to identify them from far off—by their gait, their silhouette. But in Hong Kong everything was compressed, anonymous,
tangled. Everything was the crowd, the mass. And I was always
on the outside.

"It was not the color of my skin—though that was a part of
it—or my scholarship status—though that, too, played a role. It
was the way of life. The density of the population. And its lack of
connection to nature. To anything outside of the endless canyons
and towers of man.

"But after a while, I began to see: Hong Kong, too, was connected to nature. Yes—I saw that. But what I saw, I did not love.
It was connected to nature, but only to draw it into itself. To
consume it. Hong Kong was a vortex: the ships came spiraling
into the port from all over the world, dragged in by a tide of extraction, the cranes pulled containers off of vessels that were like
enormous floating buildings, filled with everything the world had
to offer. What I saw was a flow of things—manufactured things,
yes. But also plants—vegetables, fruits from the mainland, from
all over the world. Cut flowers even from my own country. Our
coffee, too. But also—ivory.

"It cropped up here and there, at first: a chess set one of the students had, passed down from his parents. An old set of mah-jongg tiles in a shop window. Once I began to see it, it was everywhere. In offices—a tusk in a case, beautifully carved, transformed into a world of its own, worked by human hands into a chain of elephants walking trunk to tail. Beautiful, lifeless elephants carved from the destruction of an elephant, hacked into what had once been a part of a body, a tooth, a tool. A part of a life.

"Among the skyscrapers, there were also older places—little streets of cramped shops, survivors from another Hong Kong. Marginalia that had been missed by the eraser of progress. And there, in the shop windows, so crammed with clever things, there it was. My eyes found it over and over again. Ivory. Ivory jewelry, ivory stamps used to sign decrees that were meaningless now, ivory game pieces of every kind. Ivory turned into useless gewgaws, dripping with the blood of my home. It could be carved into any lovely shape they wished, but all of it began in killing. No—more than that—all of it began in killing that took place far away. That took place somewhere the people who thought of ivory as a *material* could not see. Killing that took place in an *extraction zone*.

"This was the beginning of my political life. It was a strange place for the political life of a Kenyan man to be born—among antiques shops crowded with bric-a-brac, on scholarship in a world I could spend a lifetime in without understanding. But there it was. I saw the system: cities like Hong Kong and New York and London at the center, vortexes into which the currents of trade accelerated, into which goods from all over the world were pulled. Places where things became *materials*. Where things became *commodities*. And on the other end of all of that, the places people like me were from—the *extraction zones* where the tug of all this displacement began. I saw the slave ships then, moving like shuttles in a loom across the sea. I saw the sugarcane fields and the cotton plantations. I saw the taxidermized bodies of our African animals in Western museums. I saw the rare earth metals in every terminal in every hand in Hong Kong, London, New York. I saw everything that was torn from its natural environment to become a *material*, to become anonymous, denatured. I saw all of that.

"But for some reason—perhaps because I grew up *here*, among the elephants, what caught my eye, always, was ivory. It stood out, white and gleaming among the other objects in every display—like maggots in a wound. And I understood: I know what it is like to be *from* an extraction zone. What it is like to grow up in the place where the taking begins. But an elephant knows what it is like to *be* an extraction zone. That is their history. The elephant is enormous, but it is not as gigantic as the history of human exploitation.

"I knew, then, that I would be a ranger. I would take my education back with me, and use it to put a stop to this. My parents had imagined a different future for me. They imagined me, I think, in a lab coat so white it hurt the eyes, with a patient smile on my face. They imagined me in glasses. With a pen in my pocket. They imagined me away from here—and away from here is always imagined as some kind of heaven. A place of order and well-tended gardens, where things are bought with the touch of a terminal or a nod, in stores that play quiet music. But I could no longer imagine myself in that place, knowing what I knew."

Sparks from the fire formed brief constellations in the cold air, against the more permanent constellations above them. "And that is my story. That is why I am here, Damira." Wamugunda paused, then asked, "But why are *you* here?"

Damira remembered how that question had cut into her. How she had carried it with her for weeks, trying to answer it. How it had festered, bringing doubt with it that was only really drowned when the war spread into their park, and there was no time left for thinking.

But at the time, she had just laughed: "My uncle bought me a toy elephant."

Wamugunda laughed as well. "But surely this is not the future your parents imagined for you."

"I don't think they ever imagined a future for me. So I guess I was free to choose my own."

"Ah." Wamugunda was silent for a moment. Damira watched his face, which the fire turned into shadows and planes of orange and yellow against the dark. The deepest lines of that face were rivulets, unlit canyons leading back into the night.

She returned to this memory—this place carved from oblivion—often. But sitting here across from him, warm by this fire, she was a traveler. She came from a time in which she knew he was dead. In which she knew that she had also died. She wanted to tell him, wanted to reassure him: *I do not forget, anymore. I will not forget you, so long as I move across this earth. We will always meet here, Wamugunda. This is our place.*

Wamugunda pushed an ember back into the fire. "Well, Damira—I think there are people who come from somewhere, like me. And there are people who come from nowhere, like you. And there is power in both."

THE SMELL OF fire, linking back even further, to memories of her childhood, of a biology book open on the kitchen table. Of looking up from her studies to see one of the other ancient wooden houses across the street, burning brightly despite the drifting snow.

But there were links that were broken as well. That no longer led to other memories. Were those memories still there, disconnected but whole, like planets that had escaped the gravity of their systems to drift forever in the darkness between the stars? Or had those memories dissolved over time, dissipated to relieve the neurons of the task of maintaining that connectivity?

There were memories even her mammoth mind could not retrieve from her past. So much was lost forever.

The smell of fire grew stronger. She padded forward quietly. The others sensed her effort at silence, and imitated it.

Close, now.

TEN

THE DRONE FOUND the triangle of Burlaks, huddled together against the night. At the center, two men sat at a fire. The drone circled, as if asking a question. Considering. Then it came down with a whisper of blades no louder than a bat's wings and settled on the roof rail of one of the Burlaks, from where it had a clear view of the two men.

The men spoke in low tones, in Russian.

"I don't know if she thinks of me, anymore. But I certainly think of her, out there on the steppe, living in that shape we put her in. All of these years now, and she is still out there. I've stayed away. I don't want to be a bad memory, a source of trauma. But sometimes I imagine finding her."

"What would you say?"

"Yes—that is why I never do it. What do you say to the person you brought back from the dead, then made into a monster?"

"Monster hardly seems like the right word."

"No—but I don't mean it in *that* way. I mean something singular, something *outside* of everything we have ever known. Something—someone—entirely new. We made her into a creature that has never walked this earth. But that was just a start. What has she become, out there, after all of these seasons of being what she is now? Of leading them? *Saving* them? Because that is what has happened—she has saved them. They were dying, a dwindling herd, a failed experiment. Now there are three herds. Now I am growing older, and I feel like there might finally be a future to this place, beyond me, because of her. I remember we asked the question, when all of this was failing . . ."

"What does it take to get a mammoth to be a mammoth? I remember."

"Yes. What does it take to get a mammoth to be a mammoth, and not just some hairy elephant swaying in despair in its refrigerated enclosure? What does it take to get them to know what they are, to understand how to live where they were made to live? And we have the answer, now. It takes someone who knows—or at least can imagine—what being a mammoth was like."

"It takes an expert."

"Yes—and we thought all the experts were dead. Just bones and mummies in the permafrost."

"But we found a way forward."

"No—we found Damira, and she found a way forward."

It was quiet for a moment. Then:

"Do you think she would forgive you?"

In answer, the other man drew a terminal from his anorak. He turned the screen to his companion, and showed him a number. "Kommodifi has that as the price per gram, today, of what it is calling 'New Mammoth Ivory.' NMI, for short, on the speculative index. What does that price mean to you?"

"I'm going to be honest—after months every year on horseback, wandering this wasteland, that price just means 'French Riviera' or 'Private Castle on the Dalmatian Coast.' I'm getting tired."

"Understandable. What it means to me is a future for this place. The herds are growing. Their browsing and grazing are extending the steppe, pushing the forests back, protecting the permafrost. We have wooly rhino in captivity now, steppe wolves, four short-faced bear cubs. None of those animals are identical to what once roamed here. All of them are cut-and-paste, genetic chimeras built from a scaffolding of modern animals, gestated in modern wombs, fostered by distant cousins—but they are *close enough*. We are rebuilding a world, here. A healthy world. A world where the permafrost stays, and the giants have returned. What that price per gram of tusk means to me is a future for all of that. What it means is a return on Moscow's investment. It means they will keep sponsoring this place, stay interested. Fund us. That price, and the money these rich idiots will spend, once a year at most, to hunt something in secret that they can never speak of to anyone else—to live out some fantasy and bring down a prize they aren't even allowed to keep—it's enough to make this place permanent."

"And you think Damira would see it that way? After what she went through when she was . . ." The man struggled for a word. "Back in her first life?"

Another long silence.

"I am glad I will never have to explain it to her."

"You had better hope not."

The drone rose up into the air slowly, pulling out of the fire-lit triangle and making a wide circle before it arced off into the night.

SVYATOSLAV HELD OUT his hand, and the drone dropped down into it. He placed it in its charging slot on the control headset, slid the headset back into its shock-cushioned, waterproof bag.

Myusena was forty meters away, asleep or at least prone on the ground, a shadow near the stamp of dying embers that had been their fire. The rifle was near him. Beyond him stood the mule with its load of tusks, worth more than any substance on earth. Past the mule, the stump of the tree they had hacked down and burned as fuel to stay warm for a few hours.

Svyatoslav pulled the quilted plastidown blanket tighter around his shoulders, and thought. There were rumors. Rumors that the president—that, in fact, much of the government—were dead minds, brought back in bodies the secret services grew in laboratories underground. Rumors that some of the scientists involved in the experiments were, themselves, the returned.

That was what they called them, in the stories. *The returned.* Minds brought back by some state experiment, minds copied and stored, then placed in new bodies. But it was not something

Svyatoslav had ever considered could be true. It was the kind of thing people made clips about—those paranoid clips you could tell were pieced together in basements, with images thieved from science fiction websites, old film footage, comic books. Clips where the narrators talked too fast in some affected voice, trying to sound certain of things they couldn't possibly know.

Could it be true? Was there someone called Damira, out there on the steppe among the mammoths? A mind that had once been in a human body, now . . . changed into one of them? The men had talked about it with certainty.

Yes, you could tell by the way they had spoken of it. It was true. It was a thing they had spoken about like any other fact. It was true, but he couldn't yet assimilate it into this world.

He looked at Myusena again. Asleep, probably. But maybe just lying there, waiting. Svyatoslav knew—the sum of money the tusks might bring was so enormous that Myusena would never be able to divide it between them. Even half of it was more than a person could need in a lifetime—but that made it even more unlikely that anyone would give half of it away. But there was something else that Svyatoslav knew—and he knew it because he had watched his father come home penniless over and over, smelling of sweat and drink: Myusena would never sell the tusks, and live. Somewhere along the way, they would be taken from him. He would be swindled. Killed, even. Men like Svyatoslav's father and Myusena did not get rich. They did not go and live on private islands, or send their children to university in London. No—they fulfilled their purpose: they retrieved things for others. They did the work, and were thrown away. Things like the tusks weren't just for rich people to have, or buy—the rich *already owned them.* They just needed to be handed over to their rightful owners.

There was something to the Nenets stories about how the creatures were cursed—about how they spread sickness and death. He thought of the bulls, of the sound like a sob that the younger one had made when it sank to the earth. It was not the animal, but the *act* that was cursed. The act of killing an animal in order to take something that was a part of them—and turn it into something you merely sold. It was the act of digging in and disturbing the earth that was cursed. The act of tearing the banks from streams to gouge out Ice Age corpses. Svyatoslav had seen the way the streams afterward were thick with silt and dying fish. The traces of greed swirling in the current.

Greed. This was what Svyatoslav had been thinking about after the embers of the fire died down. He could walk away. He could get away from Myusena. Even if he did not own the tusks, he could use them to buy his own life, simply by walking away from them. He could walk away from all of that wealth. Leave it. And Myusena would have to make a choice: go after him, or stay with the mule. His greed would get the best of him. It would tie him to the tusks. He would choose to stay with the mule, which would slow him down. By the time Svyatoslav had reached the ATVs where they were hidden outside the park, Myusena would be far behind. From there—free of Myusena and with transportation— Svyatoslav could go anywhere. He would have nothing, but many had started from nothing.

That was why he had been sitting here, operating the drone: he'd been surveying the terrain ahead, looking for the best route to the mountains.

And looking for the mammoths. Yes, he'd been doing that, too. Looking to see if they were in their path. If they were nearby, or moving toward them. That was when the drone had picked out that triangle of light, the three massive Burlaks parked in the middle of all of this nothing. The Burlaks were almost directly in their path. They would have come across them the next day.

The pack on the ground beside him held several days' rations, a multitool, the axe, and now his drone and control headset. It was enough to get him through. Once he had the ATV and the group's terminals, he could drive out of the taiga and then sell what he could. From that bit of money, he could buy a ticket on a train.

He saw it again—the map of connectivity, like the one his mother had shown him of the Mediterranean, the trading routes.

He could leave here, get to another place. He could follow opportunity from there to yet another place. Eventually, he would get to somewhere that was connected more widely—that had rays leading farther and farther from here.

There must be a way out into that other world.

Then he saw them.

His mind would not accept them at first—cutout shapes against the horizon, moving. Impossible.

They were already there—only twenty, thirty meters from Myusena. And despite himself, despite the fact he knew it was the worst thing he could do, that it would likely kill him, Svyatoslav cried out in warning.

He saw Myusena start, sit up. Saw him scramble like a crab through the fire, scattering its embers, trying to get to his feet. Saw the shapes closing. He saw the tusks, white in the dark, as the first mammoth reached Myusena and, with a shake of its head, caught him across the body with a tusk and threw him into the air.

Myusena hit the ground, rolled. Again, he tried to get to his feet. The mammoth bellowed. It lowered its head, and charged. It strode straight across Myusena, and when it had passed there was nothing on the ground that looked like a man anymore.

But it did not stop. It made an arcing turn, and came at Svyatoslav.

Fast. They were so fast. He had seen it before, when their hunting party had killed the two bulls. It seemed impossible something so enormous could move so quickly.

It was crossing the space between them faster than any man could run.

And he understood.

"Have you ever heard of mammoths doing that . . . attacking people like that? It was like they hunted us."

"*Mammoths are extinct, boy. Nobody knows anything about what they might have done when they were around. And these things are not mammoths . . .*"

She was crossing the space between them.

"Damira!" Svyatoslav shouted. "Damira! Stop!"

He dropped to his knees. He curled into a ball, his hands laced instinctively over his head as if that might somehow save him, and he waited to die.

ELEVEN

"YOU WILL SHOOT from a distance of one hundred meters, and no less," Konstantin said.

Anthony nodded.

"If you are shooting from the side, look for the crease of the ear. If you are shooting from the front, look between the eyes. The key is to *visualize*. Once you note the markers I mentioned, you must visualize the target inside and get it right. A mammoth brain is not a tough target to hit, but it becomes one once you bring angles into the equation. The size of the animal in comparison to a hunter already has an element of angle, but this is exacerbated by distance as well."

"I have shot elephants before."

Vladimir interrupted. "Where? How?"

"There are game parks no one knows about. High security. But the elephants are not really wild . . . they are raised in captivity, and then released. It is not much of a challenge."

There were two Anthonys. One, Vladimir knew well—the immaculately dressed, restrained, loving man who dealt with his extraordinary wealth with ease. Vladimir had not been born or grown up among the ultra-rich, by any means—but he and Anthony had been together now for over a decade. In that time, he had gotten to know their society well. There was no single, monolithic "type" among them, but there were generalizations you could make. They were all highly isolated—surrounded by financial managers, personal assistants, bodyguards, and servants of all types, forming a human fortress that made access to them nearly impossible. They were cynical about the world. This made sense: the only people who managed to storm the citadel they had built around themselves were sycophants, charities looking for money, or entrepreneurs of a thousand stripes trying to get backing for some half-cocked idea.

And they hated one another—none of them thought any of the others brought any value to the planet, though they fooled themselves, quite often, into thinking they themselves did.

Anthony was, to some degree, all of those things—except that he did not fool himself into thinking he was of any use to the world. He had been born into unspeakable wealth, but seemed perfectly aware of what the world outside the foamy, scented bath of privilege looked like. He anonymously gave enormous sums to causes he believed in, without believing he was the one making a difference—he knew it was those "actually doing the work" as he called them, who were deserving of praise. And he was not cynical about the world: he was engaged with it. He was realistic, and decent.

Or so Vladimir, over a decade of intimacy, had thought. But who was this other man—the one listening to Konstantin with a superior smirk on his face? Who was this man who was so arrogant he was certain he knew more than Konstantin—a man who had likely grown up *here*, in this place—did?

"A lung or heart shot on a mammoth is not a kill shot. They are very emotional animals and deserve a quick death. Do you understand that? It must be done correctly."

"I understand. Have you ever killed a mammoth, Konstantin?"

They were on foot, the four of them—Vladimir, Konstantin, Anthony, and Dr. Aslanov. Only Konstantin and Anthony were armed. In the silence following the question, the grass hissed at their boots.

"If you are asking have I ever hunted a mammoth—no, I have not. Nobody has, in this era."

"Have you hunted an elephant?"

"No. I do not have the wealth necessary to do such a thing."

Vladimir knew Konstantin had left the rest of that unsaid— *and I would not do such a thing if I had the wealth.*

"I have. I know how to shoot them. I only wish you had allowed me my own rifle."

Vladimir saw a glance pass between Dr. Aslanov and Konstantin. Frustration, in Konstantin's eyes. A warning, in Dr. Aslanov's.

"We have our regulations here," Dr. Aslanov said. "But I hope you find our rifles sufficient. They are of good caliber, and will be up to the task. And you were able to test-fire yours."

"Yes. It's a good rifle. And the rounds are good: super penetrators that will punch through the skull of just about anything."

He said it as if he were praising a sports car's engine, or the design of a yacht. Even the voice of this Anthony was different—the tone distant, condescending.

He should have seen it. He had glimpsed this Anthony: a shadow across the face of the man he loved, looking at the trophy photos on his secure phone. A look in the eyes, when Vladimir asked how a hunting trip had gone. Vladimir had dismissed it as a quirk—a false note in Anthony's personality—brought out by a strange, dark hobby he didn't share or comprehend. He hadn't understood, until yesterday, what it really was: some kind of split in the man. He had thought he was living with a man he understood almost fully, who had—as everyone does—a few things they hide from others.

Now he saw it differently: this was like a second person. He had been living with half of Anthony. What was truly terrifying was the thought that maybe the half he loved—that generous, decent person—was made possible only by this other half. By a man who took joy in killing. Or that the man he loved was even less than half—was nothing more than what was *left over* from this Anthony.

Or that was how it seemed, when Anthony was in this mode. A stranger to Vladimir.

He should not have come on this hunting trip. Anthony should not have *invited* him to come. To see him like this. It could destroy them.

Anthony turned to him. "Are you doing all right, Dima?"

"Yes, *bwana.*"

Vladimir didn't have to look at Anthony's face to know it had reddened.

Vladimir understood, then, why he was here. He loved Anthony—the other part of him. Anthony had thought Vladimir might come to love the rest of him, too. He had been hoping it was possible.

It was not.

"How far is he?" Anthony asked.

"Impossible to be sure. There is a spring, several hours' walk from here. It forms a pool. He was there when I rode out this morning. He may be there still, or he may have moved on. But there is plenty of forage here, so I don't think he will wander far from good water. We'll leave before dawn tomorrow. If he returns, we can set up downwind from him, and take him."

TWELVE

THE BOY SMELLED of so many things. Adrenaline exuded from him like a fog, threatening to obscure everything else. Beneath it was the smell of his unclean body: stale sweat and unwashed clothes. There were the local smells, too, from the dust and pollen on his clothes. But under all of that, the smells that had accrued in the pores of his skin, in his clothing, the lingering smells, were the smells of Damira's own people. Of their food and the way they lived. The hint of hair products, soaps familiar to her, that pulled at strands of memory.

The boy walked beside her, and spoke almost continuously. He was, she understood, hysterical with fear, and likely still in shock.

She had thought she would never hear another human speak to her, in this way. As if she were still one of them. He told her of how he had found out about her, of what he knew of Dr. Aslanov, of the other hunting party. Perhaps he thought he was exchanging this information for his life. As if he had to keep talking or she would reconsider, and crush him to death as she had intended to do before.

But as Damira walked, in the dawn light, she was only half-listening, only half-present. She knew she should be concentrating on what Dr. Aslanov was doing here, but she was drifting, distracted.

The smell of him, past the fear, was so much like the smell of her uncle Timur, just come back from his month-long shift in the Timan-Pechora oil fields. He always smelled like this— unwashed, tired, his clothes saturated with the cigarette smoke of other men, though he was not a smoker himself. So Timur was there, walking beside her. But the boy also smelled of fire, and the print of fire in her mind brought Wamugunda to her side. The boy smelled of cooked rice and fish. Cooked rice and fish was the smell of Damira's mother, and she joined them on their march. Something in the soap he must use brought back summer camps, and Alexei, the first boy she had kissed. His dirty hair smelled exactly the way her own had, camped by the Ewaso Ng'iro, when she took off her cap to wash her hair in a bucket.

The boy walked beside her, and she breathed in the layers of smells, and remembered. He walked, and he was not one person—he was an ever-shifting crowd. Timur, Wamugunda, her mother, Alexei from summer camp, her own human self, and then Musa, Yelena, a teacher from elementary school who must have used the brand of soap the boy washed his hands with. And then the man who ran a little convenience store down the street from where she lived as a child, whose jacket always smelled of old tobacco. People drifted out of and returned to the composite mass. People became other people as one memory linked itself to another, and another, and another.

The other mammoths also approached the boy, stroking the ends of their trunks on his clothing, on his face.

For the youngest among them, the ones born on the steppe, these were new smells. The older ones, Damira knew, would be remembering keepers at their enclosures. Remembering lives that were more comfortable, more ordered—but also more constrained.

Her reverie was interrupted by a thought:

They think they can kill us for profit. They think they can use *us* to pay for this place—tear our bodies apart, use our bodies for *funding.*

When she turned to look at the boy she saw Musa, his rifle over his shoulder. Musa looking up into the white-blue sky.

"Our day will come, and the corpses of the poachers who did this will be scattered by the banks of the Ewaso Ng'iro, covered in flies."

"Yes," Wamugunda said from the crowd, the angles of his face shifting, as if in firelight, though it was already dawn. "Our day will come."

Did the boy understand something? See something in her eye? Now he stood there alone. The herd had come to a stop.

"I can find them," the boy said.

Damira raised her trunk and sniffed at the air. Could she smell them? Dr. Aslanov and the others? No—there was nothing. They were downwind, perhaps. Or not close enough.

"I can help you. Look."

The boy sat down and opened his pack. Two of the younger calves came up to him and stroked at his arms and the bag as the boy drew out a smaller bag, and from it an object Damira recognized from a former life: a control headset for an observation drone. And the insectile drone itself, nuzzled in its charging slot.

"I can find them—and we can stop them."

Looking past the boy, Damira saw Kara, walking slowly up to him, her trunk stretched out, smelling. Damira knew what she was smelling, because she had smelled it herself—faint, buried in the other smells the boy was composed of. Koyon's blood, fear-tainted with adrenaline like the boy's, the smell already mixed with decay.

The smell of the boy's guilt.

Kara came up behind the boy, and raised one of her forelegs. He did not see her, but Damira watched.

Revenge. She had taught them this. We could crush this human boy like he was nothing, grind him into the earth, trample him until he barely held the shape of a human anymore. Until no one would recognize him.

He could be made to pay for what he had been a part of. For Koyon. For Yekenat.

The raised foot was like a question.

Damira did nothing.

You must decide, Kara. His death belongs to you.

Damira could smell the temporin streaming from Kara's glands. The smell of sorrow, but also anger.

You must decide.

The boy, not knowing how close death stood to his frail body, said, "I can find them with this—and maybe we can stop them before they kill any more of you. Do you want me to do that? To help you find them? If so, you can touch my hand with your trunk."

Kara stroked the end of her trunk over the boy's clothes, brought it into her mouth. Abruptly, she turned away.

Mercy. Well, *that* was not something Damira had taught them. She wondered if it would last.

Damira brought her trunk to the boy's hand.

"Good. They aren't far from us," he said. "And they don't know what happened to the poachers. Not yet. We can surprise them at their camp. We can come up with a plan. I can help you . . . confront them. We can stop them."

She touched his hand, then touched her trunk to the top of her mouth. Again the boy in front of her blurred, became so many people she had known. And she was among them, on her knees by the Ewaso Ng'iro, washing her hair in a bucket, in the days before the river was fouled with the corpses of her elephants.

"I want to help," the boy was saying. "I want to make things right."

Yes, that was what she had always wanted as well—to help. To make things right.

THIRTEEN

THEY WERE DOWNWIND of the bull. The four of them lay in the grass just over the sloped peak of a kurgan—Dr. Aslanov on the far left, and then Vladimir, and then Anthony, and then Konstantin. Konstantin had given each of them earbuds for their right ear, and his carefully formed thoughts, picked up by the black Alexander ring he wore at his temples, came through on the earbuds in a low, robotic whisper through static.

They cannot see well. He won't be able to make us out from there—but their senses of hearing and smell are so much better than ours that it is difficult to imagine. Especially in the low range, their hearing is unearthly. It is said they can feel the vibrations of another mammoth walking ten kilometers away. I believe this to be true. So what is most important is to remain still until you have your shot.

They had been still for what seemed like an hour, the flies of the steppe landing on their hands and faces, crawling across knuckle and cheekbone, vomiting stomach acid on them and sucking it back up to sample their flavors. Vladimir wished that when humankind had eradicated the mosquito, it had killed off whatever these biting flies were as well—injected viral DNA into their populations, too, crumpling their wings forever.

The Alexander that Konstantin was wearing was an old model, with a hand-held control that opened and closed transmission. The control looked like a ballpoint pen, with a button you clicked on the end of it, and a ridge you could slide from side to side with your thumb to control volume.

Vladimir was terrified of ever wearing one of those things himself. No matter how many times it had been explained to him that you had to concentrate to project a thought, that they didn't really "read" your mind, he was certain it would reveal what he really thought about people, and they would never trust him again. One of the things he was terrified of—one of the many things he was terrified of—was that people would be able to understand him. So many people said they wanted to be understood. But who could really want that?

Thank God these Alexander things were one-way.

We have all the time you need. Just wait for your angle.

Beside him, Anthony's face twitched in irritation. The barrel of the rifle drew a small circle in the bright air as he silently readjusted position.

They had been watching the bull at its watering hole for a long time now. For that entire time the bull had kept its back to them. Vladimir estimated it had been an hour, but perhaps it had been more than that, or far less—he had no reference.

He had never been so afraid of moving. He was certain he would shift, or suddenly speak for no reason at all, compelled into motion and sound by all this silence and stillness. And the bull would run away. And Anthony would hate him forever. His muscles were painfully cramped, and his body kept demanding he shift his position, but he was in terror of being the one who frightened the bull away, and so he lay even more motionless in the grass than the others.

But every few minutes the sense of wonder managed to penetrate through the pain in his limbs and the sting of the flies writhing across his knuckles, and he really *saw* it: the mammoth. The massive, chocolate-colored beast. The extraordinary length of the tusks, with their graceful curves flowing downward from the lips, angled slightly outward, then arcing back up.

It was a picture come to life, a childhood fantasy. It was a hole in time and in the world, swaying with its back to them, dipping its trunk into the pool and then spraying the water into its mouth. It was a resurrection. It was something that *could not be*—but was.

And if it shifted, if it turned this way, it would cease to be.

Vladimir had spent that entire span of time willing the bull to keep its head turned away from them.

He had seen the diagrams of the two possible shots—from the side at the level of the notch in the ears, from the front directly between the eyes. He knew the moment either of those angles appeared, Anthony would destroy this animal. This wondrous, impossible animal.

A thought kept pushing its way into his mind:

If you pull that trigger, I will stop loving you.

If he were the one wearing the Alexander's carbon-black band, he was sure Anthony would hear that thought with no static at all.

This thought was not an empty threat: it was the truth. When Anthony pulled that trigger, and that massive, hairy giant with its absurd and wonderful curves of tusk that almost dragged on the ground collapsed into death, he would stop loving Anthony.

Yes, it had been a test, bringing him here. Anthony had wanted to see if Vladimir could love *all* of him. He wanted to be loved completely, with all of his flaws. But this was not a flaw, a quirk, a personal glitch. This was intentional. This hunting was an act of destruction that had no purpose except . . . what? Vladimir could not understand it. A year of Anthony's income. A fortune. Several fortunes, for anyone who lived in the world of real money, where it wasn't counted in billions. Why this? Power? But where was the power in this—lying in the grass, led here by experts who found the animal for you, knowing the piece of technology in your hand gave you absolute control? This wasn't power.

No—it *was* power. Power was the ability to destroy without needing to. To do it not out of necessity, but as an act of pure excess. To do something to someone else simply because you could. And this was perhaps the greatest power of all: to kill something that no one else could kill.

To have a miracle resurrected—and then destroy it.

If you pull that trigger, I will stop loving you.

The bull raised its head, but not at an angle that might allow the shot. Its trunk curled through the air. Smelling.

He senses something, the Alexander's metallic voice said. *Stay very still.*

But in that moment Vladimir sensed something as well. What? An unsettling in the earth. A shifting, as if the soil shuddered.

Dr. Aslanov raised his head and turned, looking behind them. The move was sudden, and loud after the silence they had been maintaining for so long. Vladimir turned as well. When he saw them, he grabbed at Anthony's arm.

And then the gun went off.

Vladimir had never been so close to a weapon being fired before. His ears rang, and the world's sound dimmed. But he hardly noticed that. He hardly noticed Anthony's cursing, either. All he could hold in his mind was the sight of the mammoths, bearing down on them. Enormous. And very close.

Run.

It was a voice in his head, but also his own thought.

Run left. To the Burlaks. Follow Dr. Aslanov. Run!

He was already running, on ground that slid and shuddered underneath him. He turned and saw Anthony behind him. Also running, his rifle over his shoulder.

Standing atop the kurgan was Konstantin. He had raised his rifle toward the herd bearing down on him.

Anthony grabbed Vladimir's arm and pushed him forward, urging him to go faster. Behind them, they heard Konstantin's rifle thunder.

The Alexander's voice was drowned in static as they neared the edge of its range.

When you get to the Burlaks, you tell the drivers to go. Immediately. Do not wait for me.

The last thought Vladimir heard from Konstantin, small as the buzz of a mosquito against a background of white noise, was:

Damira.

FOURTEEN

"IN THE HIGH and Far-Off Times the Elephant, O Best Beloved, had no trunk. She had only a blackish, bulgy nose, as big as a boot, that she could wriggle about from side to side; but she couldn't pick up things with it. But there was one Elephant—a new Elephant—an Elephant's Child—who was full of 'satiable curiosity, and that means she asked ever so many questions . . ."

Damira was there again, listening to uncle Timur read to her. This was the gift of the mammoth mind, the elephant mind: to be where she was and elsewhere as well. To be in this present and yet inhabit the past. Not as a reverie; not the fragmentary past that was all a human mind could conjure, like a minimalist set of a play where perhaps a single well-remembered staircase, a bedsheet, and a bookcase stood out against a void of forgetting. No—she was there. Timur sat at the edge of the bed and read from the book, its plain cloth cover saying nothing of the animal wonders inside. The bookcase was there, but also the carpet nailed to the wall next to her bed, with its angular, semi-floral patterns, its smell of dusty wool. The wallpaper of the room was a faded green, with leaves suggested by paler brushstrokes. It was a forest she would enter some nights as she drifted off to sleep.

She was half-asleep now inside the warm vibrations of Timur's voice, inside the world he wove in the room. And if she concentrated she could hear the tap of snowflakes against the window, a staccato punctuation between the lines of Kipling's *Just So Stories*.

"And she lived in Africa, and she filled all Africa with her 'satiable curiosities. She asked her tall aunt, the Ostrich, why her tail-feathers grew just so, and her tall aunt the Ostrich spanked her with her hard, hard claw. She asked her tall uncle, the Giraffe, what made his skin spotty, and her tall uncle, the Giraffe, spanked her with his hard, hard hoof. And still she was full of 'satiable curiosity! She asked her broad aunt, the Hippopotamus, why her eyes were red, and her broad aunt, the Hippopotamus, spanked her with her broad, broad hoof; and she asked her hairy uncle, the Baboon, why melons tasted just so, and her hairy uncle, the Baboon, spanked her with his hairy, hairy paw. And still she was full of 'satiable curiosity! She asked questions about everything that she saw, or heard, or felt, or smelt, or touched, and all her uncles and her aunts spanked her. And still she was full of 'satiable curiosity!"

In the High and Far-Off Times. In the times when Timur had been alive, and her mother had been alive. In the times when, in winter, the snow piled so high that the narrow track to school became a white, winding canyon. In the times when her identity was still a cloud of possibilities that could begin to coalesce around any clump of dust introduced into it. When a single action—an elephant toy given as a gift—could create such gravity that the shape of her personality would begin to wrap itself around it, until it was dense enough to ignite. To become a star. To light a lifetime.

Sitting on the floor of her room, which now ran from the dark bar of rug out into a red-dust plain, Wamugunda pushed an ember back into the fire. "Well, Damira—I think there are people who come from somewhere, like me. And there are people who come from nowhere, like you. And there is power in both."

There with him by the fire that night she had been hurt by his comment, though he had not meant it as hurtful. She had felt the fragility of her position, there. He was *of this place*. She was not. She had gone to school, endless school, and then university, learning of elephants and, through them, biology and ecology, and the details of an elephant world that had once been something weightless and vague. Like Kipling's colonial Africa, which was just a fantasy-place for white Europeans to conjure with, and had nothing to do with the complexities of the real countries and peoples and ecologies of the continent it named.

But over the years, the elephant had become flesh and blood. The elephant, beginning in her life as a stuffed toy, as a story, as pictures in books, and then an anatomy to be studied, had finally become an animal she could touch. The elephant had become real. Once she had placed a hand on the skin of an elephant, under the watchful eyes of the elephant's mahout, there was no turning away. Once she touched them, she knew she would stay with them. With the reality of them, not the fantasy. First in the forests of Myanmar, weighing them and deworming them. Then here, along the Ewaso Ng'iro, in Kenya, driving transects and taking samples of blood and dung.

And then—though she tried to push those memories down—fighting alongside her friends until all her friends were dead.

Until she was dead, as well.

Because that was the truth of it: Damira was dead. This being, called Damira, remembering this room, where a child Damira was half-asleep and drowsily listening to her uncle Timur read, was not the same being as that child. This being remembering the Damira by the fire, worried she would never have a place with the friend she loved. This being was not Damira at all. Damira had been murdered at a camp ten kilometers from the red-earth patch of ground lit by the flames of that remembered fire. Damira had been hacked to pieces with machetes, and Damira's head had been sent to Kenya's president in a cheap plastic sack manufactured for holding rice.

This Damira, this being that was remembering, was nothing but a map of a woman long dead—a map folded into a new shape to fit in the mind and sinews, the massive skeleton and the sensory apparatus, of a mammoth. This Damira . . .

No, she thought. Whoever can remember is real. A being that remembers is alive, and authentic. I am here. That is enough. I am here, on the steppe. And I am here, in this room, where I was present as a child. And here, by this fire with Wamugunda, whose stories of Hong Kong I still preserve. He lives, in some way, in me.

I am changed, it is true. And even these memories are changed by what I have become. But I am here.

And Wamugunda was wrong: no one comes from nowhere. We come from our own pasts. We rise up out of our memories, and once there are enough of those memories to stand upon, we move forward with their support beneath us, drawn toward the future they allow us to conceive. We are continually shaped by our past, and we continually reshape it.

Because now, when she remembered the gift of the elephant, she remembered something strange. The gift had been a clumsy thing, sewn most likely in some factory not far from the Tomsk where she grew up, designed by people who had never seen, in their lives, many of the animals they were imitating. It was formed of cheap plush, with dark eyes of plastic imitating glass, and clumsy curves of white tusks that began to lose shape as the stuffing inside compressed.

But it had not been gray: it had been brown. She had dismissed the color, barely noticed it—after all, there were pink elephant toys and purple elephant toys and elephant toys of an acid green, so why should brown be strange?

But now she saw the loop. It was not an elephant Timur had given her, at all. That first object around which her ideas for the future had begun to wrap themselves was a mammoth.

And it was a mammoth she had become.

In that remembered room, Damira got out of bed and walked to the window. She could hear the crackling of the fire, far off, and Wamugunda's soft voice telling of Hong Kong. Further in the darkness, she knew, Musa patrolled and was not yet dead.

She came to the window and placed a hand against the pane.

Outside, the snow fell through the streetlamps in vertical streams. The herd of mammoths there in the street below were speckled with it. A newborn calf, not yet a month old, ran back and forth from mother to aunt, sweeping snow from the pavement with his trunk and tossing it into the air.

They were there, too. They had always been there. Even in the High and Far-Off Times.

"They are still there."

The boy, Svyatoslav, stood next to her. He had the visor on, and his hands were slightly outstretched, controlling his drone with small movements of wrist and fingers.

"They haven't left yet. They saw the two overturned Burlaks, and the bodies of the drivers. The one called Vladimir has been telling them they have to leave, but the one called Dr. Aslanov seems . . . I don't know. He hasn't said a word for the last hour. And the one with the rifle—his name is Anthony—he's climbed up onto the roof of the Burlak we left standing. He's keeping some kind of guard."

Temene was dragging Konstantin's jacket through the grass, back and forth, and then lifting it and slapping it onto her back, as if testing how efficient it would be at waving off flies. A calf named Borongot kept tapping Konstantin's rifle with his trunk and then loping away, turning fear into a game.

The boy, Svyatoslav, made a motion with his hand, and took the headset off. In his lap he held the Alexander, and the dropped earbud retrieved from the steppe grass.

The man had not tried to run. He had fired his rifle into the air, and waited. Had he thought she would stop? He, too, had said her name. Just like Svyatoslav had, the night before. But this time she had not stopped, even when he threw the rifle away and put up his hands. She never even slackened her pace.

Svyatoslav tried not to look at what was left of the man. The jacket he had been lying on in the grass, the rifle he had held, the Alexander knocked from his temples—these were all intact. But the human being that had been there minutes before was nothing, anymore.

The earbud had been dropped by one of the others, while they were running away. It was one of the calves that brought it to

Svyatoslav, coiled in its trunk. The same one now exploring the fallen rifle, just meters from where the dead man lay. It must have smelled the earbud, there in the grass. Svyatoslav would never have found it.

He turned it over in his hand. A shiny black seashell, curved to the human ear canal. Damira ran her trunk over it, and he looked up at her.

He almost asked the question, but did not:

Why have you let me live?

FIFTEEN

"WHAT YOU ARE telling me is that they hunted us. They came here, and attacked the Burlaks. Then, finding us gone, they followed our hunting party and attacked us."

"I don't have to *tell you* anything, Anthony," said Vladimir. "You can see what happened for yourself. While we were out there, they came here and did this. Then they found us and killed Konstantin. They will come back again, and finish us off."

Vladimir was down in the cabin of the Burlak, with its red velvet curtains, its overstuffed seats, its polished walnut paneling. The brass sconces were still there, the parquet floor, the Turkmen and Azerbaijani carpets. Even the white doily on the table, and the book: *A Journey into Mammoth Country: Your Guide to the Ice Age World.*

But now a square hole was opened in the ceiling. Through it Vladimir could see the dark, scudding clouds of evening, threatening rain. Anthony's boots clanked on the roof as he paced away and then came back. His face appeared against the clouds, sunburned and flushed.

"Why? Why would they do that? It doesn't make any sense."

"I don't know. Why do you want to *shoot* one of them? *That* doesn't make any sense."

"Where is Dr. Aslanov? I want to talk to him."

"Go and talk to him, then. He's still where we left him—up in the cab with his head in his hands. I've already tried talking to him. He's . . . he's just seized up."

"Perfect timing."

"His friend Konstantin is *dead*, Anthony. His staff—our drivers, everyone—they're *dead.*"

"We need to find the keys to this thing. They will be on one of those bodies out there, most likely."

"Be my guest."

"No." The face drew away from the square of sky and spoke from farther off. "No, I need to keep watch. And it's *you*, Dima, who are *my* guest here. Not the other way around."

Vladimir sat down at the table and put his head in his hands. It was the first time—the first time Anthony had ever reminded him about who paid. In all the years of their marriage, it had never happened. There had always been a pretense of equality, a sense that the money belonged to no one. That it was simply *there*, like a sidewalk or a tree or any of the other substances that made up the world.

Above him, the boots paced back and forth. There was absolute silence from the cab of the Burlak. Vladimir knew what he would find when he went in: Dr. Aslanov simply there, at the dead wheel of the Burlak, with his head in his hands.

Something in him had come loose. Something had broken.

Something in me is broken, too, he thought. And something in Anthony is broken. And maybe something in every single person is broken, and we just keep moving forward as if it were all normal—all of it—like insects with their heads torn off who keep crawling toward a shadow to hide in. Until that thing that has already destroyed us catches up with us, and we stop moving.

He stood up and walked to the door that separated the cabin of the Burlak from the cab. On the cabin side, the door was walnut-paneled, nineteenth century, polished to a glow. On the other, he saw it was industrial—metal covered in a textured, weatherproof black surfacing.

Dr. Aslanov still sat at the wheel, his head in his hands.

"Everyone here is dead," Vladimir said. "And Konstantin is dead. And I think we will be dead soon, too, if you don't help us get out of here."

Dr. Aslanov did not move.

"This is your fault, isn't it?"

Dr. Aslanov raised his head, and looked at Vladimir, blinking inflamed eyes.

"She won't allow it."

"Allow what?"

"The sacrifice that has to be made. To keep this place funded. To keep Moscow happy, and keep her and the other mammoths alive. It isn't what I want—it is what is *necessary*. But she won't allow it."

"*Who* won't allow it?"

"I should have seen this coming. She fought for her elephants in Kenya until the very end. She died for them. Died to save them. And I knew that, but I hadn't thought of the rest of it. I pushed that away. I pretended as if it meant nothing."

"The rest of it?"

"Yes. The rest of it. What happened the night *before* she died—when she walked into the poachers' camp and sprayed their tent with clip after clip. She killed six of them while they were sleeping. And she did it *alone*. Then she just walked back to her own camp, and went to sleep. I thought—that isn't the one we brought back—the one we brought back hadn't done that yet. She was a different person. She hadn't gotten to that point. I didn't think . . ."

"What?"

"She hadn't gotten to that point *yet*, because it was still coming. And now, that moment has arrived. *This* is her moment of rage. And she is standing outside our tent, with her finger on the trigger."

"Who? Who are you talking about?"

"Konstantin tried to warn me. He told me she wouldn't allow it. I never listened."

"Who? *Who* wouldn't allow it?"

"Damira."

Damira. That name, tinny as the buzz of a mosquito against a background of white noise. The last thought Konstantin had sent them.

It had been a warning.

SIXTEEN

ONE OF THE drivers had been crushed to death beneath a Burlak the mammoths pushed over. Vladimir hoped that the keys to their own vehicle were not in the lower half of that man's body. He did not want to contemplate what he would need to do to retrieve them.

The man's head was tilted up to the sky in a scream. The flies had found him. They crawled lazily across his open eyes.

Think of something else.

Vladimir went through the pockets of the man's coat carefully. The sun was down behind the mountains now. The shadow of mountain twilight, added to the thickening clouds, left little light. But he was working by feel, anyway. And maybe it was a mercy that there was little light: he did not, after all, want to see any of this in detail.

Nothing here.

The second driver had been caught in the open, twenty meters or so from the Burlaks. Vladimir tried not to look at what had been trampled into the earth. At some point he realized he was making a strange whimpering sound, and he willed himself to stop it.

Just go through the pockets. Mechanically. Think of something else, or don't think at all.

Okay. He just went through the pockets. And yes, there was a set of keys. He felt it.

There was nothing identifiable left of the driver.

He threw up in the grass, and wiped his mouth.

Think of something else.

But there was nothing else. He just had to keep moving.

Only one key on the ring looked like it could belong to the vehicles. Return and try it? Or look for more? How much time did they have before the mammoths returned?

The sun had gone down completely now, and the color of the grass on the steppe was unnamable, the mountains humped and crooked against the sky. He saw Anthony's pacing silhouette atop their Burlak.

Was Anthony watching him?

It's you, *Dima, who are my guest here. Not the other way around.*

No. Anthony wasn't watching him. He wasn't interested in Vladimir at all. He was up there watching the horizon. Waiting. He was waiting for them to come back.

He *wanted* them to come back, Vladimir realized. *Wanted* that confrontation.

The third driver was farther away. He had curled himself into a fetal position.

Nowhere to hide, on this almost featureless expanse. Nowhere to escape to. The mammoths must have pushed them away from the vehicles, panicked them before they could get inside. Or had they been . . .

Yes. Here was a football, crushed into the earth. They had been away from the vehicles when the mammoths came. That had doomed them.

Vladimir got down on his knees.

Was there even a bone left unbroken?

This, too, is power. Overwhelming force. Overwhelming *mass.*

Vladimir felt his stomach rise. He caught himself before he vomited again.

Yes. Here. He found the ring of keys. But what he had to do to draw it from the pulp that once had been a man was unspeakable.

"I know she must think," Dr. Aslanov had said, "that I have abandoned her, out here. But nothing could be further from the truth. I think of her every day. Without her, there is none of this. Without her, I don't think they could have lived through another season. She saved us. But what I wonder, every day, is what she is *feeling*, out here on the steppe, in this new shape. What she is experiencing. I will do anything to save this place. If only she could understand that—if I could speak to her, and make her understand. But I am not sure she would understand anything anymore. She has been out here for years. How much can be left of her humanity?"

Vladimir wiped the gore from the key ring in the grass, smearing blood in arcs on the colorless plant matter. He had pushed the thought of what he was doing so far away that it was as if someone else was doing it. He did not know who this "Damira" was that Dr. Aslanov kept talking about. A park ranger? The man was half out of his mind—at least.

In this new shape.

None of it made sense.

Vladimir looked up at Anthony, pacing like a guard on the walls of an ancient fortress, watching the horizon. Waiting for conflict—wanting it. Needing it.

After all, the fee he had paid—the enormous, unimaginable sum—was non-refundable. And he hadn't gotten what he came for, yet. He hadn't claimed the life he'd purchased.

How much could be left of her humanity?

"What use would humanity be anyway, in a place like this?" Vladimir had not said it to Dr. Aslanov then, but he said it now, to no one. "What possible use would something like that be?"

SEVENTEEN

VLADIMIR HEARD ANTHONY whistle from the top of the Burlak.

"They are coming!"

He turned and looked, but could see nothing from where he was. He ran across the short distance to the vehicle and scrambled in.

Dr. Aslanov was still behind the wheel, his head in his hands. His conversation with Vladimir had been a brief outburst. Now he had returned to his despondency.

Vladimir shoved the keys into his hands.

"I found two sets. I don't think I can recover the third. Try these. Let's hope they work."

He climbed out of the cab, and ran around to the back of the Burlak. His heart was pounding as he scaled the roof access ladder. But he felt calm, perfectly calm.

It was not the calmness that came with thinking everything was going to be all right. No—it was something else. Some kind of resignation. Everything was *not* going to be all right—and that was also acceptable. Things needed to change.

Anthony stood with the rifle raised, looking through its scope. The clouds had thickened, blotting out the mountains, drowning the last of the day. It was almost completely dark, now. What last light lay on the land drew no detail—just shape and the bled-out colors of late twilight.

Vladimir followed the tip of the rifle's barrel and saw them, coming over a rise in the plain.

They came as if emerging from the earth itself. Their bodies were the color of earth, and mounded like the earth. It was as if the soil had bulged and torn until it birthed them.

Their tusks stood out white against the dark background, so white in a world drained of color that they appeared illuminated from within. They seemed detached from the rest of their bodies, swaying above the ground, moving under their own phantom power.

He remembered his own words from a few days before—from a different world—a world in which he had not yet seen them.

There are mammoths *out there in the darkness.* Mammoths *wandering around out there. And God knows what else. We live in a world where anything is possible.*

He saw Anthony's finger tense on the trigger.

"Anthony, don't do this."

"I won't let them hurt you, Dima."

"Ant, I need you to listen to me."

"There it is. There is the angle."

"Ant, if you pull that trigger, I will stop loving you. Do you understand that? I will stop. I can't be with someone who . . ."

But the trigger's click had already come. The click, and then . . . nothing.

Anthony lowered the rifle, stared at it. He opened the bolt, and closed it again, and raised the rifle once more.

"Ant! Stop!"

Click.

Nothing happened. Anthony lowered the weapon, and stared at it.

"They wouldn't let me have my own gun. They must have done something to this one. There must be something . . . there's something wrong, some kind of safety mechanism . . ."

Below them, they felt the Burlak come to life, its engine rumbling on, the thrum of its idle through their bones.

The mammoths were close enough now that Vladimir could hear their feet in the grass.

"I don't understand it," Anthony said. "I can't . . ." He collapsed onto his knees. "I can't protect us. I can't protect you."

"This was never about protecting me."

The mammoths moved slowly. They were a hundred meters away, and then fifty, and then thirty. They came to a stop.

Then Vladimir saw a human shape. It must be Damira. She came out from among them, and walked forward.

No—this wasn't a woman. This was a boy. Just a boy, not more than fifteen or sixteen. He had a rifle slung over his shoulder. He stopped and stood just in front and to the side of one of the mammoths, one that had been slightly in the lead as they walked.

"Dr. Aslanov?" he said. "Turn this vehicle off."

The Burlak shut down with a shudder.

The boy unslung his rifle and placed it on the ground.

"Come out of there, Dr. Aslanov." And then in English: "And you two—come down from there."

ONCE ALL THREE of them were standing together on the muddied grass in front of him, the boy continued.

"We have a message for you," he said. "No more killing. No more hunting. No more. You have to find another way. No more taking from these animals. They aren't yours to take from. Do you understand?"

A long silence. Then Dr. Aslanov said, "Others will come."

"No," the boy said. "No, they won't. Because you are going to take these idiot trophy hunters back with you, and you are going to find a better way to protect this place. You are going to go back to Moscow and do what you must to find a better way."

"And if I can't?"

The boy held the black earpiece of the Alexander out to Dr. Aslanov. Dr. Aslanov hesitated, and then took it, and put it in his ear.

The boy reached up, holding the other earpiece toward the temple of the mammoth next to him. He had to reach high. The mammoth bent down, helping him. He pressed the object against the mammoth's temple.

Now Vladimir recognized it—the Alexander that Konstantin had been wearing.

And now he understood.

In this new shape.

This was her. The mammoth. *This* was Damira.

For what must have been several minutes, Dr. Aslanov stood with his head down, his palm pressed against the side of his head, listening.

Then Damira shook her head, and the boy took the Alexander away from her temple. The boy turned, and walked back among the mammoths. They turned as well, moving off slowly. Among them were a few calves, who hesitated in their curiosity, raising their trunks, inhaling the novel smells of people before trotting after their mothers.

Damira stepped forward. She brought her foot down on the rifle the boy had placed in the grass.

Vladimir heard its stock snap.

She turned to leave.

"Damira!" Dr. Aslanov called.

She paused. Vladimir watched Dr. Aslanov walk forward, his hand outstretched to her.

She turned back around. She was so close, now, that Vladimir could see the dull light of twilight catching in the gloss of her eyes. He could see that one of her tusks was broken off near the tip. The break was fresh. The white stood out against the darkness like a moon.

"I will try," Dr. Aslanov said.

In answer, Damira picked the broken rifle up with her trunk, and threw it at his feet. Then she turned away, following the others.

There was a long silence, and then Anthony said, "I tried to shoot that one. But the rifle wouldn't fire."

"No," Dr. Aslanov said. "The rifle was built to know her shape. A fail-safe. It won't fire on her. Or on any female. That was Konstantin's idea. He was always wiser than me. And less trusting of people."

"Same thing," Vladimir said.

He looked at the side of Anthony's face. It didn't matter that Anthony had not been able to kill any of the mammoths—it was enough that he had wanted to. Had wanted to, right up to the end.

The trigger had been pulled. That click, even though it was followed by silence and not destruction, had ended everything between them. Anthony's face no longer meant anything to him. It was as if, with that empty click, Vladimir woke up, and all of their years together were gone. All the feeling he'd had for this man—erased. Anthony's face was as meaningless to him, now, as the face of a stranger passing on the street.

The trip back would not end with them entering their house together. No. Vladimir would have to go farther than that, and keep going.

"What did she say?" Vladimir asked Dr. Aslanov.

"There was so much static, and some of the words . . . sometimes the human words would drift off, would change into other sounds, or patterns I couldn't understand. There weren't any complete sentences. There were . . . vibrations, calls . . . but at the end, the static faded a bit, and finally I could make out a sentence. She said, *'Our day will come.'*"

EIGHTEEN

THE FIRST SNOW of the season had a smell. It was as if the grass, touched by what would become a permanent frost, was exhaling the last sweet scent of summer on the steppe.

The snow came down wet and heavy, the flakes falling out of a gray sky banded yellow near the mountain peaks.

They had been moving all night in silence. Damira wondered what the others understood about what had happened. She had always felt a separation between them. She had always felt she knew what she needed to teach them, but did not know their minds—the limits of their understanding. They continued to surprise her, both with what they had in common with her, and what they did not.

But lately, that gap had been narrowing. Lately, she found she could better guess their wordless thoughts—thoughts that were more like shapes than sentences. She felt the *state* of her tribe, as they plodded through the darkness, like a vibration in her blood. Exhaustion. Fear. Sadness. Confusion.

Killing was something they were capable of, but it ran against the grain of them. They were peaceful animals. They did not know why they had been moved to kill, and kill repeatedly, and then moved to stop killing. They followed her as they had always done, drawn by the matriarchal bond. They went where she moved them, and they would do so until she stopped breathing. And she had moved them to kill. They did not understand it, and it hurt them and made them afraid. But she hoped it had been for the last time because she did not think she could do it again, either.

As they moved through the night, she found herself drifting in and out of the present.

She found herself once again in the kitchen of her home in Tomsk, eating rice and fish with her mother.

They ate silently, seated on stools across the table from one another in the kitchen. The room was stuffy, overheated though it was the dead of winter, claustrophobic and cramped although they were sitting in the middle of the largest forest on earth.

She was home from university, home from Moscow. She had taken the train for days. The cheapest berth on the train, the only one she could afford, in the wagons that stank of unwashed bodies, of stale alcohol and cheap food. Of cigarettes and the chemical and shit smell of the toilets.

She had suffered through it because she had been so eager to see her mother, after months of separation. But now, she found they had nothing to talk about.

Her mother had come to pick her up at the train station. They took the bus back, lumbering along streets made narrow by piles of dirty snow, the streetlights warping yellow in puddles of meltwater.

Her mother had asked her questions about her education, about the biology courses, about the other students. But she did not seem to listen to the answers.

After a while, Damira had realized what was wrong. It wasn't that her mother wasn't listening. It was that she didn't *understand* any of it. She had no responses because she had never been to university, never been to Moscow.

She had never been anywhere. She had graduated from ninth grade and then gone to a technical school to become a cook. But when that didn't work out, she started selling fish at the bazaar. And that was all she had done, for decades. When had she last left Tomsk? Damira didn't know.

She looked at her mother's red, chapped hands clutching the silverware. It wasn't she who had changed—she did not change. So it must be Damira.

When Damira had been here last, she had simply been herself. But now, it felt like there were two of her—one sitting here with her mother, eating in silence. And another *watching them eat.* As if she had stepped out of her own life.

She felt like she was seeing her mother for the first time, from that strange outside position. And her mother was just a small, dark-haired woman who sold fish at the bazaar, her hands swollen and reddened by work. A woman who rarely laughed. A woman who had never told a joke. A woman who did not read, except for sometimes glancing at a newspaper. A woman who went to bed early to be at the market early. A woman abandoned by a man she never spoke of. A woman who had raised a daughter alone, providing for her without ever, really, knowing what was inside that daughter. Or knowing that she should want to know.

Damira realized what it was in that moment, as her fork scraped the bottom of her bowl. It was an effect of education. She was *looking* at everything. *Analyzing it.* Processing it. Her life wasn't just *how things were* anymore—it was only one possible way for things to be. And there were other possibilities, now. She had ceased to be trapped here, in this stuffy room. Ceased to be trapped inside her life, yes, but she had also ceased to be able to live her life without analyzing it. Without taking everything apart to look inside.

Education had taken something from her. She could not just *be* anymore.

That was why it felt like there were two of her—one here, and the other watching. And they were both her, but the one that was here was slowly dying away, being replaced.

Her life in Tomsk had ended. And she realized she would never return here, and that she may never see her mother again.

Her mother looked up at her and said, "You've changed. But I'm so glad you're making friends."

"Maybe next time you'll come to Moscow to visit."

But Damira had known her mother would never come to Moscow. What she really meant was *I am never coming home again.*

Her mother had given her a strange look, then. It was a look Damira had not understood at the time. Later, she understood that it was the look of a mother realizing she had lost her daughter—a daughter she had never really known.

"I would like that."

Of course, she never came. And Damira never saw Tomsk again. When they spoke, from then on, it was by phone—brief conversations that went nowhere, relating the surface details to one another of worlds they could not share.

The conversations were painless. Ending them would have been an admission that they shared nothing. Continuing them came at little cost.

Her mother had understood that she needed to push Damira away, hold her at a distance. That she needed to make sure nothing bound Damira to a life that would have smothered her, destroyed her. That was the way she expressed her love for her daughter.

Her mother outlived that human Damira by many years, but had now been dead for decades.

Memories looped into other memories. She found herself again in her bedroom with her uncle Timur. With the snow tapping against the windowpane, the sound of the wind hitting the old wooden house, whistling and moaning through the gaps.

Her mammoth mind had allowed her such perfect access to the past. But now, she knew, something had begun to change. She heard, outside, behind the warm contours of Timur's voice, the mammoths walking past in the darkness. She knew that if she stood up and went to the window, there would be no streetlamps to see, no houses. There would be only the endless steppe, drowned in snow, and the shapes of her tribe as it moved, pushing away the snow to root out the frozen grass beneath, pausing and then moving on in an eternal pattern.

And she had begun, as well, to lose the thread of Timur's words. Sometimes they were not words, but only sounds, a stream of sounds like the rumble of a mammoth as it pressed against her and told her that it cared for her.

Soon enough, she knew, the walls would fade away. The window would fall into nothingness. The house would dissipate into darkness. And the bed, and the rug nailed to the wall, and the abstract jungle of the wallpaper's leaves, and her uncle's voice.

There would only be the snow, the eternal movement of the group, the warmth of her fellow mammoths' vibrations in the earth, rising through her bones.

And she would be only with them, and nowhere else. They would know her, and she would know them.

"I'll build a hut," the boy was saying, walking beside her. "I can last out the winter here, with you. I can help, if they return. We'll get through it together."

Gently—because he was so fragile, so easily broken—she lowered her head and pushed him away.

He did not understand at first. It took many pushes, and a few that were not so gentle. And still, for a long time, he trailed after the group, calling to her. Calling that name which had been hers, but that was ceasing to be.

She did not respond.

When he tried to join the group again, all of them took turns pushing him away.

He screamed, and stomped his feet. He walked behind them at a distance for days.

But eventually, just as Koyon had done a few summers before, the boy went his own way, moving farther and farther from the tribe, until his scent no longer traveled to them on the wind.

ACKNOWLEDGMENTS

THIS IS A work of fiction. As it says in the beginning of these pages, "all of the characters, organizations, and events portrayed in this novel are either products of the author's imagination or are used fictitiously." This is the truth, but there is another truth: this fiction is entangled with an ugly reality—the bloody facts of elephant poaching and the ivory trade.

I witnessed some of the impact of this trade as environment, science, technology, and health officer at the US consulate in Ho Chi Minh City, where international teams did what they could to intercept and seize the illegal ivory and horn extracted from the murdered elephants and rhinos of Africa. But I am no expert, and a brush with these issues is not enough. As with all real things in the world, I felt a responsibility to make sure I got my details correct. I read widely on elephant poaching, adding many books and articles—far too many to mention here—to my own personal knowledge of some of elephant poaching's real-world impacts.

For anyone interested in reading more about these topics, I recommend *Garamba: Conservation in Peace & War*, edited by Kes Hillman Smith, José Kalpers, and Luis Arranz, and illustrated by Nuria Ortega. This is a magnificent work, bringing together many conservation voices. Without it, many of the details in this work would not have been possible to get right. My deepest respect is for the park rangers and scientists trying to protect the elephants and rhinos, fighting a war against pointless death. Their courage is a demonstration of who we humans can be at our best— empathetic, brave guardians of our earth, and of the animals that have as much right to it as we do.

The reading on elephants was also uplifting, at times: one of the best parts of research is the way it opens up whole new vistas of meaning in the world. I learned much about the sensory and emotional lives of elephants along the way, with books like *When Elephants Weep* by Jeffrey Moussaieff Masson and Susan McCarthy as my guide, and also the deeply resonant and evocative *The Secret Lives of Elephants: Birth, Death and Family in the World of the Giants* by Hannah Mumby, which—while refusing to look away from the slaughter of elephants—also addresses the wonder of them.

For the evolutionary detail, and the science of de-extinction, I am indebted to the work of M. R. O'Connor, whose *Resurrection Science: Conservation, De-Extinction and the Precarious Future of Wild Things* was an excellent guide, and to *How to Clone a Mammoth: The Science of De-Extinction* by Beth Shapiro. For many of the complex evolutionary concepts, my touchstone was the work of Eva Jablonka and Marion J. Lamb, particularly *Evolution in Four Dimensions: Genetic, Epigenetic, Behavioral, and Symbolic Variation in the History of Life*. The inspiration for my concepts on the embodiment of meaning were drawn from my wide readings in semiotics over the years, but particularly from *Women, Fire, and Dangerous Things* by George Lakoff. At its core, this is a work of biosemiotics, and for anyone seeking an introduction to that work, you can do no better than *Signs of Meaning in the Universe* by Jesper Hoffmeyer.

Books are not only the work of a writer, and I am indebted to the talents of my wonderful agent, Seth Fishman, and to all of the people who worked to bring this book into the world: my excellent editor Lee Harris and Tordotcom publisher Irene Gallo, whose vision has done so much to bring this story and so many other stories to readers. Assistant editor Matt Rusin has had the hard job of chasing me down over the months—thank you, Matt, for making sure I get everything in on time and in the right order. My thanks to Faceout Studio and Christine Foltzer for the amazing cover. You aren't supposed to judge a book by it, but a great cover is like a beautiful door you enter a world through. Thank you as well to publicist Caro Perny, to Sam Friedlander and Michael Dudding in marketing, to production editor Megan Kiddoo, production manager Jacqueline Huber-Rodriguez, and designer Greg Collins, to Lani Meyer for the excellent copy editing (copy editors are, believe me, a writer's best friend) and to proofreaders Shawna Hampton and Amanda Hong.

I continue to be grateful to Sheila Williams, who published my first work of speculative fiction in the pages of *Asimov's*, and to Sean McDonald at MCD x FSG, who took a chance on me with *The Mountain in the Sea*, making this book and all that follow possible.

As much as I love writing, and bringing new stories into the world, it is far from being the most important part of my life. That place is reserved for my family—for my wife, Anya, and for our daughter, Lydia, without whom none of this could possibly mean anything to me at all.